LETTUCE TURNIP THE BEET

BERLIN WICK

CONTENTS

COPYRIGHT

This is a work of fiction. Names, characters, places, and incidents either are the product of the author's imagination or are used fictitiously. Any resemblance to actual persons, living or dead, events or locales, is entirely coincidental.

Book Cover Design by K.B. Barrett Designs

Editing by K. Morton Editing Services

Formatting by Berlin Wick and designed on Vellum

A SPECIAL NOTE FROM ME TO YOU

Our beautiful FMC is a digital content creator. AKA: social media manager, brand ambassador, influencer, and many other variations of this title.

I'm not sure at what point calling someone an *influencer* became a bit of a faux pas. But when you take that down to the bones, that's truly what happens. It doesn't matter if you have one follower or a million. You "influence" people. However, I think there's so much more to it than that.

You, *the influencer*, take time to create these amazing content graphics, reels, videos, and reviews. You put a piece of yourself out there everyday. <u>AND IT IS SO POWERFUL.</u>

Do you know why?

You are inspiring people. Young people. Old people. All people. You are encouraging other humans. You are showing them a part of your world. A part of your passion. It doesn't matter if it's fashion related, movie related, travel related or (my personal favorite) book related. <u>**You are so powerful.**</u> Especially those with platforms that reach thousands of people.

You can positively impact someone in less than 15 seconds, or completely ruin them in the same amount of time. Sadly, these followers can do the same right back to you.

If you are on social media, making content or just commenting on it and sharing it.
You are influential.

Some people say that social media will be the downfall of our society. Let's prove them wrong.

Be Kind. Be Authentic. Be <u>Inspiring</u>.

Social media is probably the reason you're reading this book right now. So, thank you to those who have supported my journey as an author, a storyteller and a nonstop dreamer of spicy escapades and adorable meet-cutes. I am able to write because of you.

This book explores themes around sexual exploration and is intended for mature audiences 18+.

Your mental health is important to me. Please visit my website at www.berlinwick.com for a full list of trigger warnings.

DEDICATION

To all the bookstagrammers and booktokkers that support us indie authors.

You are the real MVP's

After reading this, I hope you never look at a fire truck the same way again.

CHAPTER 1
PUMPKIN SPICE SHOULD BE A LOVE LANGUAGE

ABBY

"Hey guys, *BayAreaAbby* checking in at the Downtown Campbell Farmers Market this morning. I'll be here from 10:00 a.m. until noon near the Main Street entrance for anyone that would like to bring your items for December's community donation. Firefighters often work back-to-back days without being able to go home to their families, and it's especially hard during the holidays. Those that are interested in donating, please bring goodies, games, new appliances, and your appreciation items here. I'm gathering them now through the rest of this month and will deliver them on Christmas Eve to our local fire station to show our support. Come by and show your appreciation for all that they do. Can't wait to meet you guys!"

Lowering my phone from the selfie position, I tap the red recording button to end the video and click *Publish*, then slip my phone in the back pocket of my high waisted denim jeans.

Glancing around the market today, it's thriving, and I love seeing that. There are so many small businesses and local farmers that spend so much time unloading their products or produce out of their trucks, setting everything up for just a few hours of sellable time. But for some, it's the only way they get in-person exposure to sell their items.

"Abby!" Sarah, from one of the vendor stands, is power walking toward me with a beaming smile.

"Hey, how are you?" I respond with a smile and a wave. But she doesn't stop and barrels straight into me, wrapping her arms around my shoulders, pulling me into a tight hug.

"Well, it's nice to see you, too." I can't help but giggle.

"The post you made about my handmade soaps last week. I sold out, Abby. Completely sold out! I'm working double time trying to keep up with the demand. I've never been busier, more stressed, or happier. Thank you!" She pulls me in for another tight hug.

Moments like these are exactly why I spend so much time doing this.

"I'm so happy for you! You deserve it; your hand soaps are truly the best!" I reply, genuinely excited for her.

"I gotta get back to my station but I'm making you a basket, and I'll drop it off to you next week. Thank you so much, Abby" —she gives me a grateful look—"really."

She gives me one final squeeze then releases me before running back to her booth.

I can't help but smile at her excitement and how much my little post helped her so tremendously.

I'm just a couple weeks shy of the one year anniversary of my *BayAreaAbby* Social Share account, which has somehow blown up into something so unbelievable, I can hardly believe it myself some days.

Leaving my corporate job wasn't the smartest decision I had ever made but with the inheritance my parents left me, coupled with the massive burn out that was challenging my mental health, I decided to quit on January 1st and haven't looked back since.

With this change, I've been able to focus on some volunteer

work and most importantly supporting the local small businesses. It wasn't lucrative in the beginning, something to just fill my heart, but after a few viral videos and a couple paid sponsors—for companies I actually love to promote—now it gets me by.

Silicon Valley is a hard place for smaller companies to thrive and an even more difficult place to connect with people. With the sheer population you'd think it would be easy to meet people, connect, and socialize, but I've found the bigger the city, the weaker the community.

My Social Share page helps me feel whole with that missing piece.

Maybe I'm just trying to fill a void. Either way, it makes me happy.

"Abby," another familiar voice calls my name but this one makes me cringe. On instinct, I drop and duck behind a random booth table to hide without looking in that direction.

Shit.

Why did I just do that? He called my name, he clearly saw me. My eyes scan the ground and I catch a glimmer of something shiny.

"I hope you dropped something and you're not actually trying to hide."

"Ah, ha!" Jumping up with a penny pinched between my thumb and pointer finger, I say, "found it."

Sam's brows squeeze together "You dropped to the ground like there was a grenade thrown at you, for a penny?"

"Every little bit counts, right?" I place the penny in my pocket and dodge his gaze, as I attempt to organize the produce on a table I don't even work at.

Whose table is this anyway?

"I miss you, Abby. Please stop avoiding me." He reaches over the table and grabs my hand. There was so little intimacy in our relationship that I would crave him to touch me, so much that I would melt into him when he would. Now, it just feels like acid on my skin.

Pulling my hand back, I place it in my pocket and finally look at him.

He looks drained. Sad, even. I'd like to believe him. That he misses me. But the memory as to why he's here groveling sets me straight.

"You look tired. Late night with Sienna?" I cock my head to the side with a condescending smirk.

There's a slight twinge of guilt on his face before he rounds the table that separates us. He steps into me, pushing me back and crowding my space. I take one more step back and he follows, standing flush against me; my back is now pressed into the leg pillar of the canopy that shades us.

"I told you, that was a mistake, a one-time thing that will never happen again." He leans in closer, and I can't help but press my palms into his chest, attempting to push him back, but he's rooted to the ground, trapping me.

"Stop it Sam, let me out." Craning my head to the side, I seek more space between us but it just gives him access to the side of my neck and allows him to dip even closer.

"She doesn't mean anything to me. What do I need to do to prove that to you?"

I squeeze my eyes shut, painfully, because it hurts when I want to believe him. But I'm met with a flashback of their naked bodies rolling around in *my* bed and Sam's voice telling Sienna how desperate he was for her. How he only pretended to be with me so he could grow his following for himself and for her, too. I hate it. I hate how used I felt, how used I still feel because he never really wanted me.

The saddest part of all of it, is now everybody I talk to gets the repercussions of his actions and I hate that he stole my ability to trust people.

Before I can re-open my eyes, a hand wraps around my wrist

pulling me out of the trap and my chest is now flush with another.

A light aroma of cedar and sage engulf my senses before I peel my eyes open. It takes a moment for my sight to adjust and as it does, the vision that comes into view is breathtaking.

A man with bright blue eyes and a sharp, smooth jawline stares back at me. A mound of dirty blonde hair surrounds his gorgeous face and I'm suddenly speechless.

He wraps his arm around my waist, pulling me closer, then uses the other to cup my cheek.

His eyes bounce between mine before a sexy smirk appears and his buttery voice dances in my ear. "Hey, pumpkin."

My eyes widen at the use of the foreign nickname, then he leans down and kisses me.

He. Is. Kissing. Me.

Fireworks erupt in my belly as I moan into his mouth.

It's all-consuming and completely intoxicating.

By instinct, my hands roam up his chest and over his broad shoulders. I'm drowning in sensory overload as his lips continue to explore mine. Goosebumps erupt over my skin and everything feels so natural, so perfect.

Just then, he pulls away slowly, his forehead resting on mine and we echo each other in a breathy, "Wow."

His smile mirrors mine as we both open our eyes, recognizing the power behind whatever the hell that was.

"What the hell?" Sam's voice screeches between us like rubber on a blacktop road.

I blink back into reality and pull away as I turn around to face Sam. Instead of letting me get away, my beautiful stranger wraps his arm around the top of my chest, pulling me back into him.

"You can go," he says simply to Sam, like it's a fact.

My eyes are still bewildered but I manage a tight smile and a wave as Sam looks around like this might be a joke before he takes a few steps backwards then retreats fully. Power walking like I've never seen.

I can understand his stress. The man with his arm wrapped around me is at least six feet tall with a landscape of muscle.

Intimidating is an understatement.

After he disappears from sight, I release a long breath and turn around, stepping out of the arms of my handsome savior.

My eyes trail up his body and now that I've gotten a moment to take him in more clearly, he's utterly mouthwatering.

His stonewashed dark denim jeans fit snugly against his body, his basic white tee fits perfectly, displaying the words *Lettuce Turnip The Beet* in a column down the middle of it, and that makes me giggle.

"So, does that mean you like music or vegetables?" His brows pinch together with confusion, so I point at his shirt, reminding him of what he's wearing.

Glancing down, his dirty blonde hair falls forward, covering the sides of his face as he pulls his shirt down to read it. His lip turns up for a brief moment before he says, "Both, actually."

His smile is shy and endearing, but he exudes a confidence that I admire. He's probably in his late twenties and if I had to guess he surfs in his spare time. Not only by the look of his lean, tight body, but his beachy hair and slight golden hue to his skin.

I bite the inside of my cheek, recognizing my awkwardness, unsure of what to say next. This gorgeous man just kissed me and spared me from having to deal with Sam. I don't know what's gotten into him. He's never acted so aggressively before. Even when I found him with one of my best friends—*ex-best friend*—he didn't get that way.

"So, hey, I'm not in trouble or anything. That was my cheating ex and he's never acted like that before. I don't know what's gotten into him." I tell him exactly what I was thinking, because I feel like I need to explain myself.

"You shouldn't make excuses for him." He starts unloading

the crate that he must have carried in here before seeing Sam and I.

It's full of small pumpkins and my cheeks flush recalling the use of the nickname.

"I'm not…I just don't want you to think I'm *that* girl."

"Sounds like you left him after you saw him with another woman and now he wants you back. Looks to me like you're smart, beautiful, and deeply desired." He glances over at me, his gaze eating me up as he gives me a beaming smile. He's not stunted at all by his flaming hot compliment, but I'm on fire.

Clearly, I need praise more than I realized since my last relationship was completely void of it.

"Well…" I pat the front of my jeans, like I'm looking for something, feeling around my round curvy hips and suddenly I'm feeling a bit self-conscious. "I should probably go."

He gives me a long, languid nod.

I want him to ask me for my number but just one short month ago I swore off men for life, so that part of me hopes he doesn't.

When he doesn't say anything more, I realize he only kissed me to help me and not because he wanted to and now I'm just embarrassed and need to exit this claustrophobic canopy stat.

"Thanks again for your help earlier." I step toward him quickly and wrap my arms around his waist in a friendly embrace because I'm a hugger, and he is too, by the way he naturally wraps his arms around me and squeezes me back.

"Steer clear of that guy, okay?" he utters out loud, but not directly at me. Like he doesn't want to boss me around but he wants to make sure I know he cares.

I give him a soft nod and a stiff smile as I step out of his space. I take a few backward steps and turn around. After one small step, he calls out, "I'm here all day; you could come back whenever, you know."

I stop and glance over my shoulder and his wide smile is contagious so I call back, "I think I might have to."

With a little more pep in my step, I walk in the opposite direction that Sam went and head to the front of the market where I like to place myself to collect donations.

My phone pings with a text notification. Pulling it from my back pocket, I glance at the pop up and see "Cheating Bastard" pop up. I changed his name in my contacts so I keep that fact at the forefront of my thoughts when talking to him, although I should just block him.

> Cheating Bastard: Who is that Thor wannabe? Seriously, call me Abby. We need to talk.

It's been an eventful morning and I've received well over twenty donations for the fire station charity drop off in a couple weeks. I finish collecting all the items and load them into my car.

Closing the trunk, I stop and glance back at the canopies that line the market. Some of which have been taken down and are packing up, and a few others still selling the last of their products.

Fortunately, Sam never came back, and I feel the need to go thank the gorgeous man who helped me. Who am I kidding? I'm making every excuse to see him.

I mean, he did invite me back, right?

Okay, I'm going.

I take a step in that direction, then swivel around back toward my car.

My heart beats out of my chest as I try to talk myself into going back.

It was just a kiss, and you should thank him…again. It's easy, just go.

I swiftly turn around again and tilt up my chin. It's friendly and doesn't need to be anymore than that.

I run my hands through my dark long strands and finger my roots to give my hair a bit of a lift.

As I round the corner to the front of the market where his canopy was, it's still there, shading a table and only a few small boxes sit on top. One labeled free on the outside, an older couple steps behind the table, each grabbing the two remaining cardboard boxes as they hold a conversation placing them in the bed of a truck.

I don't see him anywhere and I realize I don't even know what his name is to ask if he's still around.

A wave of sadness hits me as I turn around and head toward my car. I'm scolding myself for not going back earlier. The other part of myself is happy that I don't have the option because that man is a heartbreak waiting to happen.

CHAPTER 2
TWO'S COMPANY, THREE'S A CROWD... OR IS IT?

ABBY

"I can't make it today." Cami's words echo through the speaker of my phone as I finish putting on the last of my mascara.

"What do you mean you can't make it today?" I ask, pausing to glare at her through the blank screen, even though she can't see me.

Cami often joins me on my community drop off days to help record everything, so the videos aren't just selfies of me and whoever I am interviewing. I always like to take time and give the donee time to talk about their services or what they do. Obviously, in this case with a fire station, it's self explanatory. But I still like them to share their stories and give them time to give people insight into their lives.

"I'm sorry, my sister has an emergency and I need to take my niece to her recital today," Cami explains with an unusually somber tone and now I feel bad I was so judgy.

"Oh no, hopefully everything is okay?" I pause, to give her a chance to share any details if she wants to, but she doesn't. "Okay, well I don't want to keep you from that and I've got to finish getting ready but call me later if you need help or anything, okay?"

"Definitely," she replies like she wants to say more, but doesn't.

"Okay, are you still coming over later for our traditional Christmas Eve movie night binge?" I ask, hopeful.

"I'm going to try, as long as everything is okay with my sister and I don't need to watch my niece."

"Sounds good. I hope your sister is okay, and I mean it, I can help with anything," I offer again, because I'd rather go to the recital, or help run errands for Cami, than be alone on Christmas Eve.

"Sounds good, have fun and let me know how it goes," she says, before hanging up and my phone beeps three times to signal the disconnect.

She's been acting a bit strange since everything blew up between me, Sam, and Sienna. She and I became really close a few years ago, then she introduced me to Sienna. I know she's feeling torn between maintaining both friendships because Sienna's been pressuring Cami to stop talking to me completely.

Which is so stupid. Sienna broke the cardinal girlfriend rule. You don't sleep with your friend's boyfriend. Yet, I'm the one being punished and outed like I did something wrong.

I glance down at my home screen that appears now that the call is over. It's a simple picture of a breathtaking sunset that I took from the Santa Cruz Beach Boardwalk. A few rides from the pier are silhouetted, just showing their outlines while the pink and orange sky glows in the background.

My screensaver used to be one of Sam and I but I picked this one as a replacement after I caught him with Sienna. Now I realize this picture was also taken when I was with Sam and it pisses me off because I love the photo so much. I don't want to change it.

I haven't seen him since the Farmers Market a couple weeks

ago. He's been texting me, but I've just been ignoring him. His absence has been hard, and I've realized, it's not because I miss him, it's because I feel so alone again.

When we first met, he made me feel so needed and desired. But now that I look back on it, the constant collaboration posts and bringing me into his newly established business was all he wanted me for. My follower count. I should have recognized his narcissistic vain personality from a mile away, but love—or what you think is love—makes you do crazy things, I suppose.

Admittedly, I've been thinking about the mysterious, kissing god from the Farmers Market more than Sam.

But, I stop myself before I go down that rabbit hole again. He's far too easy to daydream about and a productivity killer.

After cleaning my make-up products off my bathroom counter, I spritz my hair with some texturizing spray. Giving myself a once over in the standing mirror that sits in the corner of my room, I appraise the outfit I chose. Black leggings and a burgundy sweater with a black lace cami underneath. The sweater hangs off one shoulder and the color compliments my tan knee high boots perfectly. It's casual and fun, but still hides some of the extra padding in my hips.

I've never been a *skinny* girl and I've come to the conclusion I never will be. I've had hips and boobs since I hit puberty in the seventh grade and have dealt with both guys and girls making comments about both since then. Girls thinking I stuffed my bra, guys thinking it's okay to make comments about a woman's body. Incessant comments about how I should dress or backhanded compliments like, *"you're not fat, you're curvy"* or *"you carry your weight well."*

I'm over it.

I dress appropriately for my body type and over the years I've finally grown to accept it for what it is. My body is my greatest instrument and I need to be kinder to it with my words.

Ironically, the more I love it, the less other people tend to pay negative attention to it.

Grabbing my purse and keys, I exit my condo and head downstairs to the garage. I've already loaded all of the donated items into the back of my truck, last year's model of the Ford Bronco, and my first obsession in life.

When I went to the dealership to purchase one, they had this mint colored beauty still waiting to be purchased and since they were bringing in all the next year's models, they massively discounted this for me. Plus, they recognized me from my Social Share account and threw in some perks to shout out their dealership. Perks that Sam would always benefit from and it's clear as day, now, why he pursued me.

I've realized over the past couple of weeks, I'm feeling hurt and betrayed by him using me, as opposed to heartache over the loss of our relationship.

I never thought I would have to consider being used for popularity, my follower count or for benefits only something like that could bring you. But seeing how Sam treated me and what he gained, I know now that I need to be extra cautious with who I get involved with.

I start up my truck and tap my throwback playlist. Usher's *Hey Daddy*, spills out of the speakers with a melodic tone and instant catchiness.

Hm, I wonder if Usher has a daddy kink.

Jesus, I need to get laid I think.

My mind has been wandering too easily in that direction and I'm certain I need to do something about that before I start humping the nearest light pole.

I've always had a healthy sex drive, but lately, I can't seem to stop thinking about it. I even invested in some more toys to spice things up.

Jesus. Listen to me talking about spicing up my solo sex life.

Yeah, I need to throw myself back out there and stop letting the fear of what Sam did to me hold me back.

Sex toys and romance books are a decent substitute, but this can only go on so long.

The drive to the fire station is only fifteen minutes. In my research, I found that there is typically one fire station that they use for training and other stations that are strategically placed throughout the city.

Most firefighters work out of one station consistently, but in some cases if they're shorthanded, they could be assigned to work out of a different one.

I chose the smallest location since I heard people usually donate to the county's main training station or the larger ones.

I pull up and park at the curb, glancing into the tinted double doors, but can't see if anyone is in there. It always seems like stations are always desolate until all of a sudden their garage doors burst open and their sirens blare as they pull out of their stations, literally ass on fire.

Grabbing one of the boxes, I step back from my Bronco and close the door. I glance up at the clanging of metal on metal as the American Flag whips around the flagpole, the large post is buried in tan bark at the corner of the entrance. The wind is crisp and doesn't feel as powerful as it should considering how aggressive the fabric of the flag is slapping around.

I walk up to the front door and balance the box on my bent knee as I knock on the tinted glass. When I called earlier in the week, they just said to stop by anytime because someone was always here, but as a minute ticks by I wonder if that's true. I balance the box on my knee again and raise my fist to rap my knuckles against the door, then suddenly it opens, startling me.

A gorgeous man in navy cargo pants and a fitted T-shirt, that sticks to his chest like a second skin, stands in front of me with a dumbfounded look. His flawless, tan skin is only covered by the perfectly groomed beard that's long enough to cover everything but short enough to look like he just might have forgotten to shave. His sharp jawline matches his intense eyes as he silently questions why the hell I'm at his door.

"Hi, I'm Abby, I called about the social media donation earlier this week." My statement comes out like more of a question since the last few words squeak out of me with uncertainty. Usually I'm much more confident, but this man intimidates the hell out of me. Even his hair is thick and wavy in all the right places.

Inspecting his face, he looks about my age except the scowl he's currently wearing ages him by ten years.

Glancing down at the box in my arms, he finally speaks and his voice is as deep as the pinch in his eyebrows. "And so you brought us a box of kid toys and a ragged cabbage patch doll?"

I look down and I realize I should have grabbed one of the other boxes. This one I sorted with board games and the cabbage patch kid that a teenager donated with the most amazing story that absolutely broke my heart.

I stand to my full height, even though the box is heavy as hell, because I'm here to donate items and do something kind, and Mr. Grumpy Pants here is being a total dick.

"Actually, there's an amazing story behind these toys and *that* doll." I tilt my chin at it. "Also, there are more items in my car that you can help me with." One of his eyebrows lifts and a slight smirk flashes across his face so quick I almost miss it. I can't tell if he's pissed or impressed.

I set the box down in front of the door that he's holding to prop it open and sashay, with confidence, back down the pathway to the curb where my car is parked.

I press the button to open the trunk of my Ford and it beeps before the automatic door pops open as the glass top lifts. As I turn around, I see him in my periphery, trailing behind me.

Maybe he's not a heartless jerk after all.

As he rounds the corner and ducks under the glass partition, his neck cranes back and he says, "Wow."

I can't help but smile with all the donated items we received from the community.

Lots of non-perishable foods, a blender, Instapot, even an extremely expensive Breville espresso machine, tons of workout equipment, appliances and computer equipment. Someone even donated a Playstation 5. Even more of what he can't see are tickets from some of the local sports teams for different hockey and baseball games throughout the season for their off time.

He looks out of the side of his eyes then grabs a box and delivers it to the office, then comes back with a modest jog in his step.

The man might be grumpy, but wow, he's a beautiful sight to look at.

He grabs the largest box, full of kitchen appliances while I grab the last, smaller box, and we head into the main entrance.

He peeks over his shoulder behind me. "Follow me," he says, as he pushes the box that was holding the door open with his foot, allowing the door to close behind us.

I trail behind him, taking in the station as we walk through the main garage where the fire trucks are parked. There are lockers lined around the outside and tons of equipment, I wouldn't have the first clue of how to use, placed strategically in every space. The protective jackets and pantsuits I've seen only firemen wear hang in a perfectly organized manner within each cubby.

We pass through that room into another; it's a small but tidy storage room.

He places the box with random items down in the corner, then begins to walk toward me. The determination in his body language is still intimidating but his gaze, the way he looks at me, it's lacking the irritation it did before. Now, there's a desire licking through them and it feels like lava travels straight into my bloodstream.

He stops directly in front of me, his hands begin to wrap around my arms and my breath hitches at the touch. He grazes my forearm and gently pulls the box from my grasp, then says, "follow me," stepping back and out of the room.

What the fuck?

Well, I read that moment totally wrong.

See this is why I have more *friends* on social media than I do in real life. In real life, I can't seem to read cues, at all.

He rounds the corner out of the room and into another as I shuffle behind him. I have to triple step to keep up with his large strides.

As we walk through the doorway, we come into a living space area with a petite kitchen and small circular table on one side and a couch and TV on the other. I glance around the room, taking in the pictures on the wall and inspirational *Teamwork* posters, before my eyes land in the corner.

There's a large bookshelf with books lined from end to end on the top three shelves, the bottom shelves have a mix of games and a few unopened boxes of very expensive Lego toys to build.

My body naturally gravitates that way as I crouch down and pick up one of the boxes. One of these unopened Lego boxes is the same one my father had in his office that remained unbuilt his whole life. It's a *Technic* airport rescue vehicle. I don't know if he held off on building it because he knew this specific one was no longer available or because he procrastinated on it.

"My dad used to love Legos. I played with these more as a kid than I did with dolls or Barbies. They were relaxing, almost therapeutic." I smile and peek over at Mr. Grumpy Pants, who remains a freaking mute and I wonder if he can even hold a normal conversation or do more than just grunt.

I place the box back on the shelf in the same place I found it.

This place might imitate a bachelor pad by way of its basic decor, but it's spotless and immaculate otherwise.

"So, who likes Legos?" I push, because no one will stop me from talking.

He continues to unload one of the boxes, still silent, as he peers up at me, shakes his head, then finally replies, "No one really, those are just there."

"Wade does, actually."

A cavernous voice startles me, as I jump-turn around to see another man standing in the doorway.

His forearms are pressed on each side of the door jambs like he's been there just watching us the whole time. His short hair is dark all the way through except the slight graying at his temples. A book hangs from one hand while a set of black rimmed glasses dangle from the other and, um…wow.

"Who's Wade?" I ask, still a bit wide-eyed and taken aback by the gorgeous older man.

A scowl battles a look of disappointment that crosses his face, as he looks over at the mime in the kitchen. "You never even introduced yourself?"

"I didn't think she was staying long enough to need to," he replies without looking at either one of us, saying more words in that sentence than he has to me in total.

I should be offended, but somehow I sense that he's just like that all the time and I shouldn't take it personally, but I am just itching to pull him out of his crabby shell.

I return my gaze to the man in the doorway. He hangs his head down in defeat then he steps into the room, crowding the space with his oversized shoulders and way too tall stature.

"That's Wade, aka Lego lover." His lips turn up into a stunning smile as he holds out his hand. "I'm Major, and you must be Abby."

I slide my hand into his, mirroring his smile. "That's me." I return with a little too much enthusiasm. A side effect of talking into a camera to no one for too long.

My smile softens as his hand clings to mine. There's pliancy to it but a strength I can feel all the way to my bones. I stare down between our connected hands, waiting for them to light on fire with how much heat I'm feeling with his touch. My eyes trail up to his face realizing he was staring at me the entire time, his gaze now lighting my entire soul on fire.

I pull my hand away, like I was shocked, because that's exactly how it felt. Stepping back, I glance over to Wade. His body is stalled and his eyes are bouncing back and forth between the two of us.

I clear my throat and decide the only way to cut through the awkward tension in the room is to talk my way out of it.

I open my mouth to share all the details of the donated items when a third voice, a familiar voice, floats through the room.

"Pumpkin?"

CHAPTER 3
GIRLMATH: WHEN HE HAS SALT AND PEPPER HAIR AND BLACK RIMMED GLASSES, AGE AIN'T NOTHING BUT A NUMBER

ABBY

My eyes widen at the easily recognizable voice and the distinct nickname that's been on repeat in my head for the last few weeks.

My neck swivels slowly in the direction of where the voice came from, and there he is standing in the threshold of the room, sans all clothing.

One towel hangs low on his waist, while another is draped over his shoulders as he massages one side of it into his damp, dirty blonde hair. His body still drips with beadlets of water as he stands there barefoot and beautiful.

I trace the inked art over his chest and arms that decorate most of his upper body. His abs flex with the movement of his arms and I can't seem to tear my eyes away from appraising the lines of his gorgeous muscles and vibrant tattoos.

"Oh my god," trails out from my lips as a whisper. Mostly

because I'm shocked to see him, but also because he looks like he's sculpted from the Gods.

"What are you doing here?" he asks with a flirty, pleased tone, making me rip my gaze from his washboard V line, up to his bright ocean blue eyes.

"You know her?" Major asks, pointing at me.

"Yeah…Well sort of, we met a couple weeks ago but I never got her name," he replies with what looks like his signature flirtatious smile.

"What's with you kids these days not introducing yourselves to people?" Major looks between the two men, clearly not kids, but both much younger than he is.

I glance over at Wade who's standing with his arms crossed over his chest, unimpressed with this entire encounter. He releases his arms and goes back to unloading the box, shaking his head with a hefty eye roll.

Geez, he's so grumpy.

"Abby." Major holds his hand out to me, then displays the other toward the still naked man dressed in only terry cloth. "Jasper. Jasper, Abby." His eyes bounce between the two of us. "See, not that hard, right?" He smirks then joins Wade who's pulling the brand new espresso machine out of its box.

Jasper steps into the room, obviously very comfortable in his minimalist ensemble.

"Hey, pumpkin," he whispers loud enough for only me to hear.

That makes me chuckle out a smile.

"Hey," I reply.

"You didn't come back."

"I did, actually." I wince at my instant reply. I should act cool, uninterested, like I never went back.

His brows pinch in confusion.

"You were already gone." I tuck a rebel hair behind my ear,

my nerves on full display as I dip my head down to stare at my feet.

He crooks his finger and places it under my chin, lifting my gaze back up to his.

His lips part but before he can say anything Wade's voice, the one who practiced mutism when we were alone in the room, tears us out of our trance.

"Get some clothes on." His tone is laced with disgust.

Jasper smirks as his eyes flick over to Wade then back to mine.

"Why? Am I getting you all hot and bothered?" he bellows out to Wade, egging him on, as he winks at me.

"Seriously, Jasper. Go get dressed. None of us want to see that," Wade pushes.

Well...some of us do.

I internally smile to myself at my thoughts and I can't help my eyes from roaming over his chest and shoulders.

"What's wrong, Wade? Are you jealous or interested?" Jasper asks as he wiggles his eyebrow at him. I turn to gauge Wade's expression; he just rolls his eyes and shakes his head, throwing his hands in the air.

Major glances between all of us, as he pulls a skillet from the bottom cabinet. An expression I can't read crosses over his face before he looks over at me, giving me a knowing smile, and I can tell this is a daily event that he must have to deal with.

"Welcome to my world, Abby," he says playfully. "Jasper, go get dressed. Wade," passing him the skillet, "you've got break- fast duty this morning. I'll take Abby on a tour of the station before we all sit down to eat."

"Wait, she's staying?" Wade says, almost offended.

"Yes! She's staying!" Jasper calls out, fist pumping himself.

"I'm staying?" I turn to look at Major. He smiles back at me ignoring the other two.

"Best day ever!" Jasper bellows out as he turns around, rips the towel off his waist and tosses it at Wade's head.

"Jasper!" Wade yells as he pulls the damp, heavy towel off.

"What? It's clean." He waves backward with his hand in the air, as he looks back and winks at me before he strolls out of the dining room. The round, muscular globes of his ass are on full display for all of us to see, then he rounds the corner of the doorway and disappears.

My jaw is wide open but I can't help but smile because Jasper and Wade are the best frenemies I've ever seen in real life.

I turn back to Wade as he moves around the kitchen. He sneaks a couple glances my way but refuses to actually look or talk anymore. It seems like this is his normal behavior so I try not to take it personally but it still bothers me.

His face is stoic and serious, not a hint of smile behind those deep hazel eyes. His smooth olive skin makes him look like he has the perfect tan year round and he's probably got women drooling over him every time he blinks. He is really good looking, but man, he's *really* grumpy.

Wade turns on the stove and starts slicing on the cutting board. Major steps up next to me, holding his arm out toward the doorway.

"After you?" he says with a bow of his head, his respectful demeanor on full display.

"Well, thank you, sir," I reply, mirroring the bow as I peer over at him. There's a slight flinch in his eyes as a smirk appears and his tongue rolls over his bottom lip.

We walk into the main sector of the station where the fire trucks are parked. Major takes me on a full tour of the garage, explaining how they live and work in the same area and how they set up everything to be prepared for any type of last minute emergency.

For the record, they really do have poles they slide down to get to the garage. I sort of thought that was a movie myth but it makes complete sense when Major explains the timing on how quickly they all have to get dressed and in the truck.

"This is our turnout gear, the fire protective clothing we wear when we get called out." I run my hand over the dense fabric and it feels heavy and thick. I lift the hanger and can barely pull it up.

"Geez, the jacket alone must weigh ten pounds?" I state, questionably.

He chuckles. "The entire git-up is closer to thirty-five pounds, so yeah, it's pretty heavy."

I couldn't imagine running in and out of burning buildings, with regular tennis shoes and basic clothing, much less another thirty-five pounds to carry.

"Wow, that's crazy impressive. Plus, you have to deal with the heat, and possibly carrying people out of buildings. I had no idea." He grants me a bashful smile, but I couldn't be more serious. They're considered heroes for a reason.

We continue the tour and during our walk around the facility, he steals a few soft touches as he holds my hand helping me up a few awkward side stairs and guides me into the rooms with his palm on the small of my back. Each touch lights my body up like a bag of exploding fireworks, and I'm unsure why or how I can be in the vicinity of three starkly contrasting men, each making my body run so hot in different ways.

I appraise Major as we make our way back into the garage.

His dark navy cargo pants fit snug around his thick legs just like the basic T-shirt that's tucked into the waistband. My eyes roam over the smooth skin of his muscular forearms and I can't help biting my lip as I take in his strong features.

There's something about him. An aura that you can't help but get drawn to. His large frame commands a room and it's natural to follow his lead.

"How long have you been a firefighter?" I ask as I lean on the back of one of the trucks.

His lips pull back as he sucks in air through his teeth.

"Why do you have to ask *that* question? That's like asking a woman how old they are. Don't you know that's off limits?" he replies, playfully bumping his shoulder into mine as he leans on the truck next to me.

"Oh, come on, that was sly, give me some credit." My rebuttal makes him smile and, wow, he's got a gorgeous, breathtaking smile.

"Alright, you win." He sucks in a deep breath. "I enlisted in the Coast Guard when I was seventeen. I loved the routine, the camaraderie, and I was really good at it. So I worked my way up and realized how much I loved leadership and mentoring other cadets. But…all the years I was there, well, I hated the water."

My eyes grow wide at his confession.

"A Guardsman that hates water, that's an oxymoron if I've ever heard one."

His eyes widen at my use of the lingo and his head tilts to the side as he inspects me.

"My father was a Senior Petty Officer for as long as I can remember. Everyone called him Senior, and I remember thinking how strange that was because he was 'far from a senior' in age." I can't help but smile knowing how many lives he affected in such a positive way. So many people showed up for his funeral, they had to shut down the three surrounding blocks around the cemetery.

"Ah, well it makes sense why I was instantly drawn to you. You're family," he states with ease.

That's the thing about military families. They do become just that, family. The only time I felt like I had one was when we lived on base and had the support of the other families. Then we moved every couple years and lived off base, making me feel isolated and alone. It didn't help that I was an only child. Fortunately, my mother worked from home, becoming my best friend throughout my teenage years while creating and managing an online platform that she was able to sell and enjoy an early retirement, shortly before she passed.

Major senses the awkwardness in my silence and chooses to continue his story, which I'm thankful for.

"After I retired from the military I felt a little lost until someone suggested this. It was the exact opposite of everything I knew but I loved it. It had a lot of the perks the Coast Guard had that I liked, minus the water. Win, win for me." He smiles, but I raise a questioning eyebrow at him, because he masterfully avoided answering my question.

"I joined the military at seventeen, retired after twenty years and now, I've been doing this for eight years." He raises his eyebrows back at me. "Putting me at the ripe age of forty-five, for that curious little mind of yours. Double your age, I'm sure," he states, insinuating it as a question.

"Was the television still in black and white? I mean, wow, where's your walker?" I stand, playfully peeking behind him and then step around the side of the truck. He throws his head back and chuckles at my sarcasm, it's a hearty laugh from deep in his chest that travels straight to my core.

"Get back over here," he commands and whatever magic drips from his tone makes him easy to obey.

Right as my ass plops down on the bumper of the truck, Jasper calls out from the kitchen.

"Food is ready, boss."

I turn to look at him, and he's just smiling down at me.

"You like being the boss, don't you?" I gathered this from his military story and how he is so easily trained to command a room and people. Because I swear I'll do anything this man says when his gravelly voice travels through me like melted butter.

He leans into me, bringing his lips to the shell of my ear. The only thing blocking his skin on me is the thick layer of my dark hair, providing a barrier I'm desperate to keep. Because I swear if he touches me, my whole body will light on fire and we'll have a real fire emergency inside the middle of this station.

"You have no idea, princess." He touches the small of my back to guide me up. His eyes lock on mine as I stand on my Jell-O legs, confused as to how he has such an effect on me.

The amber orbs of his eyes squint a suggestive smile and I'm unsure how to read it but I don't care enough to want to try. He's easily taken my mind off, well everything, and I'd almost prefer to stay in this little bubble we've been in.

"Come on, let's go eat. Plus, if we don't get back there soon, Jasper and Wade may end up killing each other." His eyebrow raises as if sending me a secret message, silently telling me more than he should or at least making me validate my assumption.

And I wonder if those two really dislike each other or if there's something more than meets the eye.

CHAPTER 4

PLEASE NOTE FOR THE RECORD: HOT COFFEE NASAL ENEMA'S HURT LIKE A BITCH

ABBY

The mouthwatering aroma of a homemade breakfast wafts through the air as I walk into the kitchen.

I can't help but lift my chin and close my eyes, taking in the scent that reminds me of the weekends I would wake up to a gourmet breakfast cooked by my mother.

As a single, working mother, she didn't have much time during the week. She was busy raising a teenage daughter and trying to work enough to support us. She balanced it well by working as much as possible during the week so the weekends could be dedicated time for us to spend together. And it always started with a hearty breakfast and puzzles in the morning.

It was a routine that stuck with me, even after she passed. But my cooking skills, no matter how hard I try, are nothing compared to the delicious meals she made.

She made scrambled eggs look sexy.

I'm lucky if I don't accidentally burn my cereal.

"Oh my god, it smells delicious." I round the kitchen island to the stove and peer into the skillet.

Grilled butternut squash, kale, asparagus, zucchini, and onions are resting in a large oversized skillet, sautéed to perfection. There's a large pan full of scrambled eggs and a plate sits on the side of the stove with perfectly crisped bacon cooling next to a bowl with a towel draped over it.

Nosily, I tilt my head as I pinch the corner of the towel and lift it. "Homemade biscuits?" I practically squeal.

"Did you make these?" I look over at Wade to find him blushing.

He nods with a tight expression but there's a flash of pride behind his eyes.

"You cook?" I ask, kicking myself because I should have asked him a more open ended question if I'm ever going to get him to talk. So, I'm shocked that he answers me with words.

"Yeah, we all do. It was my turn to make breakfast today." His tone is stern, but not quite as harsh as earlier. "Except Jasper, he hardly cooks anything, and if he does, no one really wants to eat it." There is a slight roll of his eyes and now he just sounds annoyed.

"Oh, you like it, you control freak," Jasper chimes in as he sets the table. "I donate the food, you cook it. Plus, you hate eating other people's food."

"You only donate it because your parents have a farm," Wade insinuates.

"It's still my food."

"Not food you pay for."

"Neither do you."

"Enough," Major interrupts, as his eyes bounce between the two of them and they quiet down immediately.

This seems to be an ongoing and very regular event between the two of them.

I peek over at Jasper as he throws a grape up in the air then catches it in his mouth. He doesn't seem to be bothered by the banter at all as he turns and gives me a beaming, gorgeous smile that I contagiously mirror back.

When I glance over at Wade, he's watching Jasper annoyed, but with an added expression I can't read.

Silence deafens the room and the awkwardness feels thick. Maybe because I'm here, or maybe because it's just normal between these two, but I usually talk into a phone screen with no response so I'm used to creating conversation with less than this.

"So, what kind of produce does your family grow?" I ask Jasper.

"We grow everything, it just depends on the season. In the summer we're known for our tomatoes. Oh, and our strawberries and blueberries are very popular," Jasper adds.

"Mmmm Hmmm," Major moans as if he took a bite of food, but when I glance his way he's just humming in memory of said berries.

"Yeah, those are his favorite." Jasper chuckles. "But fall is a huge season for us. We grow everything, from the leafy greens to beets and potatoes. Oh, and my personal favorite, pumpkins." He winks at me.

My cheeks flush as I bite my lip because his flirtation is over the top killing me in the best way.

"And all the food that Wade cooked is from your farm?" I ask, impressed.

Jasper walks over to the kitchen to double check everything Wade cooked and nods. "Yup, everything except the bacon and some of the ingredients he made the biscuits with."

"I'm so excited to try it," I say as I walk over to where Major is standing. "Thank you for inviting me to stay."

"Anytime," he says like a promise, as he gestures to the table for me to walk to.

There's nothing fancy about the seating arrangement. The wooden table is circular and fits four people, six if you wanted to squeeze in two more chairs. Yet, he pulls out my chair with a slight bow and holds out his hand as a formal invitation for me to sit.

"Thank you, sir." His lip twitches as I take a seat and he places a napkin over my lap as if we were getting ready to eat at a Michelin star restaurant.

Wade walks over with a plate in hand and places it in front of me. With my short stature and his tall one, my face sits right at his hips in this position and I glance up, giving him a shy smile as I tuck a loose strand of hair behind my ear.

His eyes solidly connect with mine and for the first time I can see the golden hazel flecks in his dark irises and they're absolutely stunning. He studies me, his eyes dropping to my body then back up to my eyes and there's something electric and undeniable between us.

Jasper plops down on the seat directly across from me and rips us out of our trance.

Clearing my throat, I'm able to croak out "thank you," before Wade glares at Jasper then turns on his heel, walking back toward the kitchen island. He grabs the other plates, placing one at each setting then sits down next to me.

Even with the rallying between Jasper and Wade, there's a togetherness with the group as they all sit down with the plates full of a home cooked meal and it feels so comfortable.

More comfortable than it should.

Everyone eases into conversation with each other and I'm able to ask a question here and there about the station and how the schedule for the firefighters work.

I knew they worked long hours and often stayed at the station. Apparently these three are often paired together and work twenty-four hour shifts, then have forty-eight hours off, then repeat that schedule. But somewhere in between they get a few days off in a row before going through that cycle again.

"That must be tough on your families," I ask, digging for

more information about their home life, as I take my first bite of biscuit and moan out loud.

"This is *really* good," I say through a mouthful of the soft, flakey bread. "It has the perfect amount of crispness to the outside but it's so soft." I moan again.

As I glance up, all three guys are looking my way. Jasper with a beaming gorgeous smile as he bites the corner of his lip. Wade's jaw is clenched but not in an angry way, and Major stares at me with his fork hovering over his dish and a glint in his eye.

Our eyes connect and the fireworks tingle against my skin. How is it possible that I'm equally attracted to all three of these men who're drastically different from each other?

I clear my throat, placing the loaded biscuit down on my plate.

"I'm quite the foodie," I confess embarrassingly, as I finish chewing my food and use a napkin to wipe my mouth.

"That's good, because if you weren't Wade's food would have definitely turned you into one," Jasper admits as he slaps Wade's shoulder, leaving his palm there giving him a small squeeze before letting go.

Wade glances down at where Jasper's hand was, shifts in his seat, then continues to eat silently. Major's eyes flick between the two quickly before he catches me looking at him and grabs his coffee, taking a small sip.

"Gracie loves all the leftovers you bring home," Major adds as he peers over at Jasper.

My eyes widen. Oh, god. He has a girlfriend.

My cheeks flush as I recall the kiss we had at the farmer's market and all the flirty banter earlier today. Now, I'm feeling totally embarrassed. I grab my coffee and take a large swig as I attempt to hide behind my mug.

"She sure does, total heifer she is." I snort and the liquid lead feels like lava as it flies out of my nostrils.

"Ow, oh my god. Ow." I laugh, embarrassed, but squint in pain.

Jasper is chuckling behind his hand and Wade stands, grabbing a napkin to hold in front of my face as his other hand delicately caresses my back.

"Are you okay?" Major asks.

"Yeah, oh yeah, I'm good. I'm good," repeating urgently, like it was no big deal. I wipe my face and the spots on the table, as I attempt to recover from my nasal enema.

I thank Wade silently with my eyes and a soft, sheepish smile. He leaves the napkin with me as he takes his seat again, giving Jasper a sharp look.

"You shouldn't say that about women, Jasper, especially your girlfriend," I whisper, accusatory.

I recall the way I felt when Sam would comment on my weight whenever he had the chance. Especially when I was eating.

Don't eat all that, it'll go straight to your ass.

Have you checked your weight lately?

Calories in, calories out.

It was constant.

I'm curvy, I have a little extra padding in a few places but I've come to appreciate my body after years of berating it.

Am I skinny and fit with a six pack? No.

But, I eat balanced meals, exercise when I can and do as much as I can in moderation. I hate that there's so much pressure on women to have this ideal body type that we could strive a lifetime for and still never be satisfied.

"I would never." Jasper leans forward, dipping his eyes to meet mine that are fixated on my plate. "Gracie's my cat," he says assuringly, like he can sense the words I've heard before.

"Oh." I huff out a laugh.

"Yeah, she's perfect." He chuckles back. "One eye, two and a half legs, loves food and cuddling."

"Loves food and cuddling, huh?" I repeat with a giggle. "I just got part of my slogan for my dating profile."

There's an awkward pause between everyone before Jasper chimes back in.

"Lily loves your cooking too, doesn't she Wade?"

"Let me guess. Lily is your lizard, that's missing its tail and loves chocolate," I reply as I peer over at Wade.

"She's my daughter."

CHAPTER 5
OPPORTUNITY KNOCKS. TEMPTATION LEANS ON THE DOORBELL

MAJOR

"Oh, sorry. It's just we were being playful, I didn't mean to…" She pauses. "How old is your daughter?" she continues.

"She's three," he replies with a small smile.

I'll never forget the day we opened up the garage bay doors and all of our eyes landed on the car seat that sat perched up against the brick wall of our station.

None of us heard the baby crying until the garage doors were opened, which led me to believe she was sleeping peacefully until she heard the creaking of the metal when the overhead doors lifted.

Wade's face fell instantly when he recognized the seat. Lily's name came out in a frantic whisper as he ran over to her, dropped to his knees, unbuckled the strap, and pulled her into an embrace.

I witnessed him realize so much in one moment.

His girlfriend left him.

She safe surrendered their own child to *his* fire station.

He was, in the blink of an eye, a single dad.

Lily immediately calmed and cooed in his arms like she

knew, too, and something shifted in him instantly. From that moment on, nothing else mattered but Lily.

Wade might be a moody pain in the ass most days, but he's loyal and loves with his whole heart. He's a caretaker and wears the weight of the world on his shoulders.

I continue to watch as Abby asks questions about Lily and how easily Wade opens up about her. He's usually reserved and shares nothing, but there's something about Abby that intrigues all of us and I see a side of Wade I haven't seen before.

He has a crush on her.

Jasper does, too. It's harder to pinpoint because he's a natural flirt, but there's a nervousness to him that I typically don't see in his free-spirited personality.

My gaze bounces over to Jasper who's listening to Wade tell a story about Lily's love for Lego demolition and he's just as interested in his story as Abby is.

These two fight nonstop but they're the best guys I've ever worked with. Jasper would run into a burning building to save a pet spider if he had to, thinking nothing of his own safety if it meant saving someone or something else. He's both brave and spontaneous, a bit of a loose cannon but he's selfless.

Wade is more calculated and the most strategic of anyone I've ever met.

The two together are like oil and water, but somehow combined, all of us make the best team in the field.

Lately though, I've noticed a difference between the two of them. They fight worse than ever, but the tension isn't the same.

The feeling is…different.

There's an underlying sexual tension and I'm unsure if I'm just reading too much into it or if my gut is leading me in the right direction.

Jasper *likes* Wade. And the nicer Jasper is to him, the more Wade pushes away.

But I don't think he wants to.

"Major." Jasper's voice surprises me as it pulls me out of my thoughts. "Abby wants to do a video for her socials."

"Oh, right. Let's do that in the garage. We can have the trucks in the background." I glance over at Abby, raising my eyebrows to ask her approval.

"Sounds perfect." She bounces out of her seat with excitement and I can see how giddy this makes her. She must be a natural giver and it makes me wonder how much of that translates over to her in the bedroom.

She's called me *sir*, twice. Not that I'm counting. But both times it lit my dick up like a billboard in Times Square.

I wonder if she's naturally submissive, giving herself to someone else or if her giving nature likes to be in control while she pleases.

I can't help but watch her hips sway as she walks toward the door and my neck attempts to follow her around the corner.

Jasper chuckles, and it's the second time he's pulled me out of a stupor while wrapped up in thoughts of Abby.

"Make your move, Maj." He tips his chin in the direction she headed.

It's not often I feel distracted by a woman, but I can't seem to keep my head on straight or my imagination for that matter.

I'm flustered by her and even more embarrassed that the guys can sense it. So, I say the only other factual thing I can think of.

"I'm too old for her." I stand, picking up my plate and walk over to the sink, rinsing it before placing it in the dishwasher.

"I doubt she thinks that," Jasper replies, placing the rest of the dirty dishes in the sink.

Ignoring his comment, I reply, "I'll clean up. You guys go help her set up for the video. I'll be right there."

Wade and Jasper glance at each other, like they're both thinking the same thing. But they say nothing, thankfully, as they follow Abby to the garage.

I know they're confused because neither one of them has seen me show any interest in a woman since my divorce, so this is an entirely new situation for them. Hell, it is for me, too.

It's been years since a woman has caught my attention, yet she comes sauntering in here, with her cocoa colored eyes and bright sunshine smile and I'm a puddle at her feet.

Placing my palms on the corner of the sink, I lean into it sucking in a deep breath.

She's a gorgeous temptation and a dangerous one, considering it's obvious all of us are into her.

My interests are different though. My ex couldn't understand it, hell she didn't even want to try, but something in my gut tells me Abby won't be nearly as judgmental as she was.

Shaking my head, I pull myself out of my own thoughts yet again today. I need to stop this. "Get yourself together," I whisper to myself.

"Maj, we're ready!" Wade calls out.

Grabbing the towel, I wipe off my hands and head toward the garage.

We'll get through this video and thank everyone for their donations, then send Abby home. We have too much work to do and it's Christmas Eve. I'm sure she has other things to do than spend it here with us.

Plus the longer she stays the more a temptation she'll become for all of us.

CHAPTER 6
A LITTLE COMPETITION NEVER HURT ANYBODY

JASPER

"If it's alright, I'll start recording at the front of the fire truck, telling everyone where I am. Then I'll walk down this side showing everyone the garage as I walk up to you guys standing behind all the donated items. Will that be okay?" Abby asks, as she fiddles with her phone.

It's definitely more of a statement than a question. I can tell she does this often and is more than comfortable in front of a camera. She should be, she's absolutely stunning and no matter what she's doing it seems like people are easily drawn to her.

I know I am; I was the moment I saw her under my canopy stuck behind the douchebag that had her pinned in the corner.

Thinking back on the moment, I definitely didn't plan to kiss her but I'm so glad I did. Not only did we stick it to her cheating ex-boyfriend, but it was the most unexpected sensation I've ever experienced.

It wasn't just a kiss. It was like the planets aligned in one life-defining moment, eclipsing all others in the matter of milliseconds.

The way our lips fit together before my tongue peeked out to explore hers. She tasted like strawberries and whipped cream, the perfect combination of addiction.

I haven't been able to get her out of my mind and now I understand why her ex was trying to trap her in a corner that day.

"Sounds good," Major replies with a bit of uncertainty in his voice.

I don't know what happened between breakfast and now but he's suddenly reserved and standoffish, which is so unlike him.

Wade helps Abby arrange some of the boxes and I watch him interact with her. Normally he's a total moody prick, at least to me he is. But with her, he's sweet and caring. Much like how he is with his daughter.

I walk past them and he grunts, like some pained animal.

I mean don't get me wrong, he's always grumpy, but at least he's helpful and kind to Abby right now.

Placing myself next to Major, his arms are crossed over his chest with his back up against his locker and one leg crossed over the other. I mirror his body language as I lean up against the wall next to him.

His eyes are fixed on Abby, like he's drinking every inch of her in but still can't quench his thirst.

"Someone has a crush," I state vaguely.

"Yeah, he does," he replies evenly, not taking his eyes off Abby and Wade.

"I meant you."

His neck whiplashes in my direction and I plaster a tight lipped smile on my face.

"Don't act like you don't," he replies.

"*I'm* not. You are."

"I meant Wade."

My smile fades as I open my mouth to reply, but have nothing to say to that.

Because, it's true. I just didn't realize anyone else was catching on to it.

I suppose if anyone would have noticed, he would. Major *sees* everything.

"Yeah, well we're both gun shy to show our cards, aren't we." I give him a knowing look, because I'm a vault and would never divulge anything he's shared with me in confidence, but I wish he were more open about his desires so he could actually find happiness with someone, instead of hiding from it.

Me on the other hand, I'm an open book with everything in my life. My sexuality has never been an issue nor a big topic of conversation. All the guys at the station know I'm bisexual so it's not like it's a big secret and when people do ask, I say what I've always said; *I'm attracted to people in general, to the connection, regardless of gender.*

There are a few judgmental expressions that quickly get covered up, but in general, most people are more than understanding. However, when you're attracted to someone of the same gender that isn't gay or bisexual, well, that can create some awkwardness I'm not willing to risk.

I love this station and the guys I work with, and it's not worth making anyone uncomfortable.

I hate that I can't help my attraction to a guy who wants nothing to do with any type of relationship—with any human— much less another man.

Sometimes, a moment will pass between us and I can't help but think he feels it too.

Then he gets angry and treats me like shit for days on end, until he finally comes back around, just to repeat the same cycle.

But, Wade has a side that not many people see and I get the pleasure of witnessing when the brick wall that surrounds him isn't fortified like Fort Knox. The few select times he lets it down and opens up to people, he shows a completely different side of himself, and in the rare moments I've seen it, my mild crush grows deeper.

He's showing that side to Abby now and I can't say a wave of jealousy doesn't roll over me.

"Alright, ready?" She glances over at us and we both kick ourselves off the wall in synchronized motion like we were just waiting at her beck and call.

Which we pretty much are.

She turns on her heel and walks toward the front of the garage, and I swear all our eyes are frozen on the exact same spot. Her hips sway naturally behind the skin tight leggings that hug the curves of her gorgeous body like a second skin.

Puffing my cheeks I blow out a long breath, needing to calm my currently rising blood pressure.

"Yeah…Yeah, Yep," echoes on each side of me as both guys agree with me.

"I think I'm going to kiss her," I announce, watching Abby talk animatedly into her phone, as she makes her way toward us.

"What?" they jinx each other again.

Nothing like lighting a fire under both their asses.

They don't know that I've already kissed her. They don't need to know that.

But, they do need to know I'm going to make my move, and these two are nothing but competitive.

CHAPTER 7
WELL, THAT WAS AN UNEXPECTED ASSIST

WADE

"Thanks again to everyone who donated to this great cause. Please share any local businesses or nonprofits that I can show some love to so we can continue to support our local community. See you guys soon!" Abby pulls her phone closer to her as she taps the screen with a beaming smile.

God, she's stunning.

I find myself with a rare smile, that I quickly shed, as she finishes her video with an excited squeal.

"That was great you guys!" She places her palm over my forearm excitedly.

My gaze makes its way to where she's touching me and I can't help but shift my stance, because just that little contact has more blood rushing to my groin than I'd care to admit.

She senses my discomfort and pulls away urgently, embarrassed, like I was disgusted by it. Which is the exact opposite of how I feel and want nothing more than to pull her entire body next to mine.

Instead, I do what I normally do and scowl, clenching my

jaw for good measure, because now I'm pissed that my natural body language gave her the wrong idea.

I blame Jasper.

Actually, I blame Jasper for everything.

Because being around him…just… *fuck*. Pisses me off.

I can't believe he said he's going to kiss her.

But, I believe that's exactly what he'll do. Because he's like that. He goes after what he wants and doesn't care about what other people think. Plus, he's completely unafraid of rejection.

He's far more charming than all the guys at the station and can flirt with a shovel and it would somehow show interest.

Me on the other hand, I can't flirt to save my life. And, even if I did, I'd have nothing to gain from it. I have a daughter to focus on and way too much responsibility to get into a relationship with anyone. I haven't even gone on a date in well over eighteen months.

Although, that's not because of a lack of time; I know my sister would help with Lily if I wanted to go out. I just have no desire to.

Abby bends over to push one of the boxes to the side of the garage, and any remaining blood flow that helps me think straight flows directly to my half hard cock.

Jesus, it's been so long that I can't even control myself when an attractive woman *bends* over.

As she stands to her full height, which isn't much—she can't be taller than five, three—she grabs a jersey from the box and tosses it over to Jasper.

Jasper reaches up, snatching it with one hand. He gives her a playful wink before throwing his other hand behind his neck, grabbing the back of his shirt, pulling it forward over his head.

I swear the guy is always half naked.

My eyes peruse the hard lines of his body and I swallow thickly. His lean frame is cut in ways I've never seen with intricate tattoos that trace over his chest and shoulders. He even has a goddamn eight pack that trails underneath his low hanging cargo pants and my eyes roam further down his body, stopping dead center at his fly.

My assumption that he goes commando is spot on when I see the mushroom crown of his cock through the fabric of his pants.

Now I can hear my own heartbeat whooshing in my ears as my lips part and I dart my tongue over my bottom lip. I have no idea why I have this reaction to him every time.

Jasper pulls the jersey over his head, the shift of his body breaks the connection I had and I rip my gaze away only to find Abby staring at me, her own lips parted as she bites on that plump bottom lip of hers.

Fuck.

She looks curious and really confused.

I need to get the hell out of here.

"I'll be back," I state and turn without making eye contact with anyone.

Taking large strides I make my way out of the garage, down the hallway, and step through the threshold of my bedroom, closing the door behind me.

Running my hands through my hair I press my forehead into the wall and exhaust all the air from my lungs.

Abby started this, from the moment I opened the door this morning and she was leaning over that heavy, awkwardly sized box with her full breasts pushed up against the cardboard, and her thick, dark hair draped over her tan shoulders, looking like a goddess.

Then seeing Jasper shirtless, not once but twice today.

I don't like men, I internally remind myself.

I have no idea why every time he's around I have this uncontrollable visceral reaction. I always force myself to hold back from these rampant thoughts of him, his body, his flirtation, but I only succeed for so long until I can't control the urge, like right now.

Reaching down, I fumble with my belt before I tear open my zipper and push down my pants. Wrapping my hand around my already hard cock, I squeeze rough and angry, because I'm fucking pissed I'm doing this again, thinking of the one person I shouldn't be thinking about.

Squinting my eyes shut, pre-cum pours out the tip and it's been too long since I've given myself any attention due to shame of the thoughts I had the last time I relieved myself.

"Fuck you, Jasper," I whisper, feeling the distinct tingle at the base of my spine, knowing just the thought of him touching me sends me spiraling over the edge so goddamn fast.

"I fucking hate you." Gritting through my teeth as I glance down between my legs envisioning him there, looking up at me.

I'm angry, so fucking angry. At him, at myself. Abby for initiating this sensation. At everything.

But I need this. I need this so bad.

Closing my eyes, I think about Abby joining him on his knees, both of them begging me with their eyes for a taste, licking their lips like they can't wait for it. "Fuck yes, both of you take my cock," I fantasize out loud, Jasper leaning in as he wraps his lips around the tip and I groan, throwing my head back, "Goddamn it Jasper, fucking take it."

The door clicks behind me and I jump-turn, as I attempt to reach for my pants but topple over onto the bed.

My stiff cock bounces against my stomach as a string of pre-cum leaks out the tip.

Covering myself with my hand, I glance up to see Jasper standing in my room with the door closed behind him. His hands are splayed out in front of him like he's protecting himself from an incoming attack.

I'm heaving, my breath is short and labored, not only from how aggressively I was fucking my hand but from the fact that he probably fucking heard me.

I close my eyes, squeezing them shut, then reopen and he's still fucking there.

Goddamn it.

He's frozen as he stares at me, his eyes bouncing between my eyes and my cock. I can see his chest rise and fall with calculated breath, like if he makes one wrong move the entire room will blow up.

It fucking feels like it will.

Any minute now. Please, take me and put me out of my misery.

Fuck, this is awkward, and embarrassing.

If he starts being his typical self and makes a joke right now I might kill him. I can't take it.

"Please, just get out." I manage to say the words but they come out defeated. My entire body slouches except my stupid cock, standing full mast, not defeated in the least.

"Don't…" Jasper starts to talk but I interrupt him.

"Don't freak out?" Oh, I'm freaking out.

"Don't…stop. Please," he pleads.

It's only then I glance down seeing the bulge behind his pants and desire burning in his eyes.

"Please," he says again and my cock twitches. "Keep going."

Fuuuck.

I don't want him knowing the things I think about while I touch myself. If he stays he'll think I want that or like it. I don't…It's just a reaction. It's just physical.

Just because I think of something while I touch myself doesn't mean I want it in real life. It's just a simple fantasy. But, if he stays. No, no…he can't stay.

I shake my head back and forth as I glare back at him, pissed he's seeing me like this, vulnerable but so goddamn desperate.

I can't move. My body is like a stone statue even though my mind is reeling a million miles an hour.

"Please, Wade. Just pretend like I'm not here." A pained look crosses his face before he pleads again. "Please."

My jaw slacks open with his words and I can't hold back. I squeeze my eyes shut and wrap my hand around the length, pumping it from base to tip. The pre-cum lubricates my shaft, as I continue to stroke myself, the wet slapping sound echoes through the air between us.

My breaths shorten as my climax builds and I finally open my eyes, because as much as I don't want him to see me doing this, I want to see his face when I come.

His eyelids are heavy, matching his labored breath and the look behind the lust in his eyes ignites my entire body on fire. "Fuck," he hisses, as he places his hand over the front of his pants and his hips push forward in slow motion, like he can't help but move because he needs the friction.

But he won't dare step toward me, I can see the worry in his expression that I'll stop.

Because I should fucking stop this.

What the hell am I doing?

I slow my pace and start to release my grip. But, he steps back, urgently slamming his hand over the top of the light switch and the room goes pitch black.

"Don't fucking stop." His tone is demanding this time. There's no desperation in his voice like before, no question.

I hear his footsteps draw closer, then flinch when I feel his hand wrap around my wrist. His grip is soft but tight enough that he doesn't allow me to pull away.

Turning my hand over, he spits in my palm. "Keep going. I want to hear you come all over yourself."

Jesus Christ.

I can't see him. I wouldn't know he was here if it weren't for the heat of his hand around my wrist, that woodsy sage scent that follows him everywhere and his desperate, heavy breath that matches mine.

My hand doesn't move, until he guides it over my lap and my fingers naturally wrap around my cock. I grip it with a needy moan, but I remain frozen, unsure of what to do, until he begins to guide my hand up and down with his.

I grunt at the foreign sensation of someone else's pace—a man's masculine grip—while my fingers continue to squeeze the full length of my shaft. His saliva coats the tight skin around my cock, and the excess moisture creates slurping that sounds a hell of lot like someone sucking my cock. I close my eyes and return to the vision of Jasper in front of me, mouth wide open as his lips wrap around my cock. The sight rips the orgasm straight out of me as if I had no preparation for it and I lose all control.

"Fuck. Fuck…Fuck." I beg, whimper, plead. I have no idea what other words spill out of my mouth.

My entire body is riding a high I can't describe and even though I'm sitting down the room spins. I lean back onto the bed, my hands falling to my sides as I catch my breath.

A minute goes by, a few seconds. I can't tell. It's still dark and I can finally hear again after feeling like I was in a room with an exploding pipe bomb.

I sit up in the darkness but the scent that's so distinctly him is gone and the sensation that someone is here is missing, too. I stand up, pulling my pants up enough so I'm not shuffling to the door and switch on the light.

He left.

He fucking left.

CHAPTER 8
JERKING OFF YOUR STRAIGHT FRIEND IS WELL WORTH THE CONSEQUENCES. I THINK

JASPER

I left.

I just fucking left.

But I had to. I had to before I made him do something he would've been way too uncomfortable doing.

I round the corner of the hallway and my entire body melts into the wall as I lean against it.

Fuck.

I peer back around the corner to see if he's opened the door but it doesn't even look like the light is on yet.

Another thing I couldn't manage to do…turn the light back on. Because I know the moment I turned on that light, reality would hit him as to what just happened and he would hate me, and even worse, hate himself.

I could tell by the way he was talking to himself when I walked in there. Scolding himself really.

But then he told *us* to take him.

I didn't know who he meant at first, then he said my fucking name while tugging at that thick, gorgeous cock of his and I froze.

Watching him please himself while he called out my name. "Fuuuuuck," I spit out, as I squeeze my eyes closed, tapping the back of my head against the wall.

I should've turned on the light. We could have talked about it.

No. I shake my head.

He would have thrown me out, not knowing what to do or say and it would have been awkward as hell.

I'm better off leaving until the moment is right.

But he probably fucking hates me more than ever now.

I peek around the corner again, because fuck, I want to go back in there. Demand he accept that was the hottest fucking thing we could have ever done and get me off in return.

Years. Years I've fantasized about him. Jesus, it was better than I ever imagined.

He was thinking about *me*.

I can't help the lopsided smile that appears on my face, knowing I had that kind of effect on him.

I am definitely taking my shirt off around him more often.

A door slams down the hall and when I peek around the corner for the third time, a sliver of light shines through the slit at the bottom of the door.

Soooo…he's pissed.

Maybe I should go back now.

"Jasper?" Abby's angelic voice calls from behind me and I turn, almost as suddenly as Wade did when I caught him in the room.

"Hey." My reply is urgent.

Another thunderous sound barrels out from Wade's room and she cranes her neck to look down the hall.

"He just needs…some time." I reply as we both hear drawers slamming.

"Did I do something?" Her brows pinch together.

"No," I step toward her, "not at all." I have an urge to touch her like she needs comfort and reassurance. Or maybe that's me after what just happened.

I stare into her gorgeous chocolate eyes as I trail my hand over her arm and reach for her hand. Her fingers are wrapped around the handle of a bag and she lifts it up showing me a large oversized box placed inside the plastic, her smile a mile wide.

I squint, confused.

"It's a special edition Lego fire truck, I thought he'd like it and I was hoping to build it with him." Her reply is adorable and certain, like she's already made up his mind for him. "I thought we could build it and he could take it home to Lily. I know she's too young to play with it, but maybe just display it somewhere for her later." She shrugs and there's a tad of shyness to her tone I haven't heard before.

Wade loves puzzles and games, specifically building stuff like Legos. That's how he spends most of his free time and it'll probably help get him out of his head, especially if he has a partner.

"You know," I glance down the hallway, "I think he'd really like that."

"Yeah?" she asks, needing that same assurance I did a few seconds ago.

I nod and smile, keeping my gaze locked on hers.

"Want to come with me?" That uncertainty is back in her tone as she glances down the hallway like she's worried of rejection.

"I gotta help Major with some stuff, but Wade will be happy that you're checking in on him." I give her a chaste kiss on the cheek and wink, as I step around her heading down the hallway in the opposite direction. He's less likely to be a prick if it's just her.

Stopping just before I round the corner, I turn around and call out, "just…you know, knock first."

CHAPTER 9
PARTNER LEGO BUILDING = DIRTY TALK

ABBY

*J*ust knock first.

Of course, I'm going to knock first. Who doesn't knock?

I shake my head with an unavoidable smile because Jasper has an aura about him that pulls it out of me against my will.

His easy going personality is a sharp contrast from Wade's, but there's something about Wade that I can't seem to shake.

The moment he told me about his daughter, it was like he came to life. Sharing all the things they do together and everything she likes.

It's crystal clear how great of a father he is and even more obvious how much pressure he puts on himself to be present for her.

I pause in front of his door, hearing the rustling of wooden drawers behind it.

I have no idea why he ran off like he did.

The video we did was great. All of the guys were totally engaged while recording and afterward, I was proud to give them the hockey tickets and jerseys that were donated to the station for the entire season. They all seemed so excited, with the exception of Wade, who sort of just scowled at me and Jasper.

Apparently Jasper is a huge hockey fan so he was more animated than everyone combined and proceeded to get half naked to try on the jersey.

A nice little perk for my hungry little eyes. And I couldn't help but take in every inch of his toned body while inspecting the lines of ink over his chest. I think I may have been drooling a bit.

It was fun, playful banter. Until I saw Wade in the same needy state I was staring at Jasper. Then he just stormed off.

I thought maybe there could have been something between them at one time but Jasper mentioned Wade hasn't had a girlfriend since Lily's mom left and that was almost two years ago, which was right around the time Jasper started working here.

I shake out my confused thoughts because I could overanalyze all of this until I'm dead and buried. All I know is the crush I had on Jasper from weeks back has yet to fade and I'm finding myself in quite the predicament with more than one crush.

Three in fact.

How is that even possible?

Raising my arm, I ball my fist as I attempt to knock on the door but it swings open before my hand can make contact. My arm flies forward hitting nothing but air, while Wade stands in the doorway with his jaw clenched as tight as his hand, making a white knuckle grip on the side of the door.

His eyes immediately soften, along with his tight shoulders that slouch slightly as he lowers his hands to his sides.

"Hey." A question and a statement.

"Hi," I reply.

A moment of silence passes as he dips his head forward and glances down the hallway, his brows furrow, then stands to his full height as his eyes meet mine again.

"Expecting someone else?" I ask playfully.

"No," he says, defensively.

"Okay, I was just…" I pause, because this is awkward. I realize being direct is clearly a requirement in communication with Wade. So, I lift the bag between us, pushing it into his chest before stepping through the door.

"I want to build this Lego for Lily and you're going to help me."

I pass by him with my chin held high as my eyes glaze over the immaculately organized and clean room. It surprises me considering it sounded like the zombie apocalypse invaded here earlier with the aggressive banging that resonated through the hallways from this room.

There are two full size beds on each side of the room, with a small reading chair and a two person table placed in the corner.

"Ah, this is perfect." I walk over and pat the tabletop as he stares at me, bag in hand. He finally shuts the door shaking his head, but not enough to hide a small smirk that he attempts to cover up.

"Okay, sweetheart. You're the boss."

"No, insert it here. Yeah, push it in. Yup, right there. Yeah, that's good. Ooh, perfect." My mind goes in the gutter with his direction as Wade praises my Lego building work, peering over at me with a smile.

The past hour has been a complete one-eighty from how Wade acted during breakfast and in the garage. He's been calm, kind, and *so* patient.

It's been a long time since I've built a Lego so there were moments of confusion. Wade stepped in calmly, reviewing the instructions and guided me through it. His understanding and patience level is seriously unmatched.

I had to refrain from wanting to toss the thing across the room.

"So, Lily loves the rain, huh?" I ask, as I peek at the instructions and snap on another piece.

"She does. It rarely rains but when it does, she runs and grabs her bright purple rain boots, and once those things are on it's full blown mayhem. I've never known anyone to love an actual mud bath, but she's out there practically shoving herself in human size potholes."

I toss my head back and laugh. "It can't be that bad. She's a kid, of course she's going to get dirty."

He cocks his head at me with a lopsided frown and raised eyebrows. Slipping his hand in his pocket he brings out his phone, tapping on the screen, then turns it around to face me.

A photo of an adorable baby girl with bright platinum hair wearing purple rainboots and a yellow jacket is laying stick straight in a muddy puddle. Actually, I can't say it's really a puddle. There's definitely more dirt than water and there are large blobs of thick mud plastered all over her body. She's got a beaming smile as her bright blue eyes look at the camera with pure joy.

"Oh my, she's living her best life," I reply, grabbing his phone and pinching the screen to zoom in on her adorable face.

"She is." He chuckles. "I've never been a fan of the rain, but she makes me look forward to it," he says with a grateful smile and I can see how much he loves his little girl.

"She's lucky to have you." He glances up at me and doesn't say anything, but I can feel how much he appreciates what I said.

"Is her mom around?" I ask, curiosity winning over my willpower.

He shakes his head, "She left when Lily was just a baby." He glances over at me with a sad smile, but it doesn't feel like it's for him. It's for Lily. "But, my mom and sister help out a lot when I'm at work, so she's got amazing women in her life."

"Her dad is pretty amazing, too," I reply with a smile, because I think he needs the reminder.

I swipe out of the zoomed in picture and the next one slides on the screen. There's a little heart at the bottom indicating it's been favorited in his phone. I tilt my head as I look at the photo. It's a picture of the garage from earlier. Jasper's entire body is in full frame with his back to the camera watching me as I walk up the side of the fire truck, looking into my phone with a smile.

"Oh, I— I was going to post about the donation." He grabs his phone from my hand, clicking the side button making the screen go black, as he shoves it back in his pocket.

I pause for a moment, and wonder if I should ask why it was in his favorites folder, but decide against it.

"Tag me in it when you do, so I can share it. The community donation part of my page is my favorite thing to do." I smile and he nods, holding the Lego truck in his hand, he turns it from one side to the other as he inspects it then places it on the table and pushes it toward me.

The table is dramatically less clustered now that we've fitted most of the pieces.

I pick up the truck, glance at the instructions and look up at Wade holding out the last piece in his palm. He saved it for me, which I find oddly endearing.

Pinching my fingers together I pick the final piece out of his hand, snapping it on, then tilt my head to the left and right as I push into each side, ensuring it's snug.

"We finished it!" I stand excitedly and round the table to show him.

He turns to face my direction as I walk up to him with a proud smile. I haven't built any Legos since my dad passed and my heart somehow feels a little fuller.

I hand him the fire truck, and he reaches forward to grab it. Our fingers overlap and the warmth of his touch as he grazes his fingertips over mine makes my breath hitch.

Our eyes connect and electricity moves between us. My heart rate picks up and the sound beats loudly through my eardrums.

I shift my gaze down and realize I stepped right in between his legs when I walked to his side of the table and we're so close, my body is almost flush with his.

Gently pulling the Lego from my hand, he places it on the tabletop, then returns his gaze back to me. My tongue darts out to lick my bottom lip and my teeth graze over the bottom pulling it into my mouth.

His hazel eyes bounce between my eyes and lips before his thumb and finger pinch my chin, making my lip pop out.

He licks his own lips as he trails his thumb over the plump skin of my bottom lip. He caresses it and alternates pressure as he moves it back and forth while his eyes bore into mine. It's like he's debating a mathematical problem and the only way to solve it is never take his eyes off me. Even though his gaze is trained solely on my face, I feel him everywhere.

Lowering his hands, he trails them down my arms, creating goosebumps in his wake. It's soft and sensual, kind and calm, exactly like his behavior the entire time we've been building.

Both palms now press against my hips and his fingers bite into my sides, gripping firmly. His touch is hard but comforting, and somehow makes me feel safe…and incredibly turned on.

He leans in slowly, simultaneously pulling my hips flush with his and we're only inches apart.

My eyes flicker to his lips and back up to his eyes. They're darker than they were before, the honey hazel are now a deep amber and I'm addicted to the richness of them.

Our breath is heavy as he dips his head slightly to the left as I tilt mine to the right. We're both cautious, as we lean in closer to each other. His lips are a feather width away. I purse my lips softly, as he grazes his over mine, then pulls me forward crashing our lips together.

His hand reaches up to cup my cheek, pulling me deeper into

him as he moans and squeezes his eyes shut. Like he's been dying to do this his whole life.

"You feel so good," he whispers in disbelief in between kissing me. And he's right, because he feels just as good. Our kiss is powerful, needy and all consuming.

I moan and nod, wanting to tell him the same, as my fingers tug on the fabric of his shirt.

Knock. Knock.

Jumping back, I'm startled and completely out of sorts. I got lost in the moment, being completely swept away by him and my mind is reeling. I look at Wade then at the door, wide-eyed and a bit worried because I shouldn't be here doing this.

"Are you guys done building that Lego yet? Major agreed to play one of the board games down here but only if it's all four of us. Let's gooooo," Jasper says with excitement as his voice fades down the hall.

An awkward moment passes between us before we both let out a soft chuckle. I feel like a teenager that just got busted in her room with her boyfriend and I think he probably feels the same.

"Well, I guess we should head down." I pat my leggings like I'm looking for my keys. Clearly confused and out of it.

"Yeah," he nods as he stands, "I'm just going to clean this up, I'll meet you down there."

"I can help." I step forward but he interrupts.

"No…no, it's okay, I…um, need a minute." He smiles with raised eyebrows.

A breathy Oh, passes between my lips before I can hide my smile.

I head toward the door and sneak a glance back at Wade. The strong lines of his back peek through the fabric of his shirt and he picks up the extra pieces from our fire truck. His dark brown hair is a little disheveled, looking like how I feel but there's a happiness to his body language that wasn't there earlier and I can only hope I had a little something to do with that.

Wrapping my hand around the door handle, I pull open the door and take a step through it.

"Hey Abby," Wade calls out and I pause to look back at him, "she's going to love this." He holds up the truck with a beaming smile and it makes me want to give him a thousand more kisses so he can give me more smiles like that one.

CHAPTER 10
HERE, HOLD MY MORALS. I'VE GOT SOME QUESTIONABLE IDEAS

MAJOR

I'm out of my goddamn mind.

Abby was going to do the social media video then head home. I had that set in my head so I didn't act on my baser instincts, but no. Instead, she felt bad about Wade storming off and wanted to cheer him up. She grabbed a donated Lego set and waltzed up to his room like she knew exactly what to do.

Then when Jasper came back he was acting weird. He was uncomfortable, constantly looking toward the staircase, waiting for…something. It was odd and I've never seen him anxious like that before.

Finally, after an hour he had enough waiting and talked me into playing a board game then ran up to grab them.

He's annoyingly persuasive and I usually have much more willpower when it comes to doing something I don't feel like doing.

But, it doesn't have anything to do with not wanting to play a silly board game and more to do with the fact that I want—and don't want—more time with Abby.

I want to pursue her, but so do my guys. I should back off,

but my body is pushing me in one direction while my mind is pulling me in the other.

There's just something about her. Not just in her magnetic personality but something is telling me to take the leap with her. To see how open she is…sexually.

Considering how my ex-wife responded to me opening up to her about my sexual desires, I'm a little gun shy dropping that bomb in the form of a question to Abby.

Jasper has opened up to me in the past. Hell, he's open with everyone but he's told me about his escapades with both men and women and I know this is something he'd be open for.

He's offered more than once to be the exhibitionist in my voyeur fantasy. I've considered taking him up on that and we came close once when we both went out for his birthday a few months back.

By the end of the night, the girl that we were both interested in had far too much to drink for either one of us to feel good about taking her home. So, we opted to get her an Uber and he and I went our separate ways. But, I've been daydreaming about fulfilling that fantasy ever since.

Admittedly, my thoughts have gone beyond just watching. Even though I don't have any desire to be with another man, I wouldn't have any issues joining in, taking turns pleasing a woman. Especially after getting my fill of watching them together.

But, it's always just been thoughts, wet dreams, wishful thinking. Never something I've thought of seriously pursuing with anyone specific, until I saw Abby today. I've never had a woman bring out this craving more than she does. And seeing her with both Jasper and Wade has my mind reeling in more taboo thoughts than I'd like to admit.

I have no idea what's going on between Jasper and Wade, but seeing the push and pull with them lately, and that goddamn sexual tension between each other, has me wanting a front row seat when something finally happens.

Add Abby to the mix, "Fucking Christ." I can't help but say that out loud. It would be like Oppenheimer testing the first atomic bomb. So tense, *so* explosive.

A pipe dream, I'm sure.

But surprisingly, I'm actually more secure in Abby's response than I am Wade's. Even though my gut tells me Wade wants exactly what I'm dreaming of, he's just too fucking stubborn to open up.

I know his ex-girlfriend hurt him and I know he juggles so much responsibility. But, if I could just get him to loosen up a bit and potentially act on the crush that I know he has for Jasper—and now Abby—I think that would help him in so many ways.

My back is toward the door as I place all the board game options on the coffee table when I hear Jasper return.

"Hey Jas, take it easy on Wade if he doesn't feel like playing. I'm sure he's just working through—" I stop when I turn around and see Wade standing in the doorway, waiting for me to finish that sentence.

"Working through what?" he asks calmly, factually.

I crane my neck to look behind him confused, because I was certain Jasper would return first.

"You know how insistent Jasper is. I was just trying to tell him to not push too much," I reply, hoping he won't ask anything more so I don't need to open up that can of worms with him right now.

"What am I working through?" He's staring at me, jaw clenched and his gaze is serious, silently demanding an answer.

I could lie.

But I'm not going to.

"Working through your crush on Abby…" I reply and pause as his face softens. "And Jasper," I add, and his face tightens again.

I can't help the passing look of disappointment that crosses my face.

I get it, I do. He's not comfortable with his feelings. Maybe he doesn't understand them. But I'm giving him the perfect chance to talk about it.

He must see the plea in my face to open up, to say anything; that I'm here to listen to whatever he wants to say out loud because he nods.

My eyes saucer in surprise.

He's staring straight down at the floor, avoiding all eye contact but he's *actually* nodding.

His Adam's apple bobs as he swallows thickly and finally says, "Yeah."

"Okay," I say cautiously. "Do you want to talk about it?"

"Nah."

"Okay, let's try that again." I pause as I walk around the table toward the kitchen trying to act as impassive as possible. "Tell me about it."

Grabbing two bottles of water, wishing they were beer, I toss one in his direction and he catches it squarely in his hand.

I screw off the top and take a swig, keeping my eyes trained on him, with hope that he's not shutting me out already.

He looks around the room, then back at me and down at the floor. Finally huffing in defeat before speaking.

"Nothing can happen, so it doesn't matter."

"Fuck that." I don't typically use any type of profanities, especially at work, so my direct response has him snapping a look in my direction.

Because, it does. How he feels fucking matters.

"Your feelings matter, a whole hell of a lot actually, so don't diminish them like they don't. You're used to ignoring how you feel and prioritizing others. Lily specifically," I add.

"I'm not gay," he says quickly.

"Neither is Jasper," I quip back. "Gay, straight, bisexual,

asexual, magical purple unicorn, whatever variation, it doesn't fucking matter." I want to get through to him. I'm practically begging in my tone. "Your feelings," I point at him, "they do matter."

He's not used to anyone fighting for him. He's only ever focused on what his daughter needs and always puts himself last.

"You can still care for Lily and give her the best version of yourself, regardless of your sexuality."

He glances around the room again, placing his hands on his hips and huffs out another deep breath.

Wade's natural communication skills are pretty much non-existent, so talking to him is the same as talking to the plastic bottle tucked in my hand, but I know he hears me.

"What would you do?" His eyes finally meet mine. "Would you act on it?"

I pause a moment, thinking back on all the things I refrained from sharing in my marriage. Years of pretending to be someone I wasn't to appease someone else.

I'm forcing him out of his comfort zone, it's only fair I do the same to myself.

"My wife left me because I wanted to share her." His brows furrow at my confession. "I wanted to open up our marriage and explore sexually with her. More specifically I wanted to watch." I swallow thickly before standing up straight. "I wanted to see her with other men."

It's a kink I don't understand. I wish I did because it makes me feel like a horrible partner, so I just shrug when Wade glances over at me as he absorbs the details I just shared with him.

He's confused, but the look on his face is less judgmental than my ex-wife's. He at least doesn't seem disgusted at the idea like she was.

I think back on how horribly that conversation went the moment I told her. Maybe I already knew I was losing her and thought it was a way to save our marriage, or maybe I finally felt comfortable telling her because I knew it would give her the excuse she needed to leave me.

"Have you and Jasper—?" Wade hikes his thumb over his back, cutting himself off from finalizing his question.

It's a fair question, considering how sexually carefree Jasper is.

I shake my head. "No, no. I don't have any desire to be with other men, but I'm not against a threesome. For me it's about witnessing the pleasure and," I take a deep breath, "I can't tell you how many passing thoughts I've had today of that exact scene with the three of you." I finally spit it out.

"Oh…" His expression is pure shock.

He runs his hand through his hair, his eyes bouncing between different spots on the floor as he probably tries to recap the memories after my divorce, trying to piece it all together.

"I had no idea about your wife, Maj. You guys were so happy and it suddenly ended, I never wanted to bring it up because I knew it was a tough topic."

I shrug. I'm not trying to dumb down the situation but what happened, happened. It was hard but it was harder pretending to be someone I wasn't.

"Everything worked out like it should have. I don't have to hide who I am from the person that should love me unconditionally. Hopefully, one day I'll be able to find that again."

My statement is about me, but it's meant for him.

A look of understanding crosses his face. He opens his mouth to reply but laughter from the hallway kicks both of us out of the conversation, as Jasper and Abby walk through the doorway.

CHAPTER 11
WELL, THAT ESCALATED QUICKLY

WADE

"Hey, hey, hey," Jasper announces as he and Abby walk into the living space.

"Well, look who finally decided to join us," Major says, playfully but still with that bossy undertone he likes to use on everyone.

I make my way further into the room as my thoughts run rampant after the conversation I just had with Major.

He's a voyeur.

I'm more than shocked by this. Major loves being in charge. He loves being in control of everything. I can't imagine him just sitting there watching.

There's no way he'd just be quiet and watch. He would be the director, still telling everyone what to do.

My cock twitches at the idea of that. Being told what to do to Abby…to Jasper.

Fuck.

I shake those thoughts away as I mindlessly make a snack platter for everyone.

I usually make mini snack platters with a bunch of fruit and crackers for Lily and I find myself just making a bigger, cooler, adult version of one.

I use a variety of fruits that Jasper brought from his farm. Pears, pomegranates, kiwis, and oranges. Along with different colors of grapes spread across the platter. I place aged cheeses and nuts in between the bunches of produce and even though I prefer the summer fruits, this platter isn't half bad.

My eyes stray over to where Jasper and Abby are sitting on the couch. They're so close to each other, her leg is flush against his and they're both carefree and laughing.

Abby looks up, catches my gaze and smiles and I can't help but smile back. She turns away and begins to sort through the games on the coffee table while asking Major about some of them.

I can see in my periphery when Jasper looks in my direction, but I'm going to find my inner toddler and pretend like I don't see him. Maybe I can hide behind a curtain or duck slowly, elevator style, behind this kitchen island.

Jesus, listen to me.

I want to be pissed at him for not only walking in on me like he did, but worse, walking out. He literally just left me in a dramatic, vulnerable state with my confused thoughts…in the dark.

I understand why he did it. I hate it, but I understand it. There was nothing but awkwardness that was going to come out of him staying in that room with me.

And thankfully he left because Abby showing up was the best *date* I've had in a long time.

At first I thought Jasper sent her to check on me, but she came on her own freewill and brought that damn fire truck Lego. She might as well have brought a heart shaped Lego, because she's quite literally rebuilding mine.

I've felt more emotions in the last few hours than I have in years and my mind is having a hard time keeping up with it.

Abby's kiss, Jasper's touch, and Major's confession. It's a lot to take in.

"Can I help?" Jasper is suddenly standing next to me and I flinch at the sound of his voice. I was so lost in my own thoughts I didn't even see him get up. A pained look crosses his face quickly before he covers it up.

"Sorry," I confess, "I didn't see you there."

"Looks good." He leans over inspecting my carefully curated snack platter then snags a piece of fruit ruining the perfection of said platter.

"Hands off." I can't help the lopsided smirk as I attempt to smack his hand away.

"Nope." He pops the P then leans in and whispers in my ear, "Can't help myself." A full body shiver runs over my body with those three little words. Stepping back he winks, then rounds the kitchen island sitting back on the couch next to Abby.

I roll my eyes and smother a smile at his uncanny ability to make me feel at ease even with the intensity of everything that has happened in the last couple of hours.

I guess he's always had that going for him—making everyone feel comfortable and cared for, a characteristic that I've always been attracted to but would mask in the form of jealousy because I've refused to accept that attraction.

I stand, watching the three of them talk about their favorite board games. Abby and Jasper are sitting next to each other on the three person couch, while Major took a seat in the chair opposite the coffee table. Thankfully there's one more chair next to Major and across from Abby and Jasper so I'll have the comfort of the coffee table separating us.

My body is too tense to squeeze in between the two of them. I continue to watch and mindlessly sort the food as Abby and Jasper sneak glances my way and it's obvious that Major can't keep his eyes off Abby.

I grab some crackers, pick up the plate, and take a deep

breath. Whatever happens, happens. Taking a page from *Jasper's manual on life,* I need to be more open, less rigid, and not so hard on myself about *all* of this.

I already put too much pressure on myself when it comes to Lily and far too much pressure on how I perform at work. Which we should. People rely on us.

But I know that I need to relax a little and not take every passing moment so goddamn serious.

I suck in a deep breath and head over toward the couch, putting the snack platter down on the coffee table with the bowl of popcorn I made. It's nothing extravagant but it'll do for board games, I suppose.

"Wade, wow. This looks amazing!" Abby beams as she picks up a sliver of a pear and slides it over her tongue, chews then moans. "So good."

We all pause a beat, taking in every last soundwave of her delicious moaning.

"No, pumpkin," Jasper says, leaning closer to Abby, "that moan is what was good." He reaches past her, picks up an orange slice, then hangs it over her mouth. "Open."

Abby's eyes bounce between me and Major as we both sit like statues watching the interaction.

A tight bashful smile crosses her face before her teeth graze over her bottom lip. She breaks out into a full smile then slowly, so sensually opens her mouth and pushes out her tongue.

Jasper sucks in air between his teeth, resulting in some type of animalistic hiss before he places the small juicy wedge on her tongue.

Abby closes her mouth over it, inadvertently getting the tip of Jasper's finger. He lets out a husky growl, before clearing his throat and pulls his hand away, trailing it down her chin.

Jasper's lustful eyes flutter between her eyes and lips, as he grips the fabric of his pant leg. Grabbing it as if to prevent himself from wrapping his hand around her face and pulling her into him.

I peek over at Major and I don't know if he's actually breathing. Like his breath got stuck wherever his thoughts are.

Me? Well, I'm shifting in my seat trying to hide the raging hard on that I shouldn't have.

"Well, now that we all know the only way Abby is allowed to eat her fruit," Major shoots a confident wink in Abby's direction and her cheeks flush an adorable shade of pink, "Shall we start a game?" Major finishes completely composed, like he wasn't just a frozen gargoyle a moment ago.

"That sounds like a great idea. What game are we playing?" Abby's cheeks are still flushed as the question leaves her lips, a shy glance bouncing between the three of us.

Jasper's body is still turned in her direction. His lustful eyes bore into her, the lids of his eyes fluttering between her mouth and eyes. His chest rises and falls heavily as if he's trying to maintain his oxygen levels.

He seems to be in a bit of a stupor and I don't know that I've ever seen him speechless, the man talks to everyone, incessantly actually. So, the fact that he hasn't said anything in the last sixty seconds says something.

"Scattergories?" I throw out my vote.

But Jasper quickly vetoes that, spitting out, "Truth or Dare."

CHAPTER 12
THERE'S NOTHING LIKE AN ADULT GAME OF TRUTH OR DARE

JASPER

Please say yes. Please say yes.

I silently plead with the desperate look on my face.

I can't see myself but I know what I look like. A pitiful adult male, one inappropriate thought shy of premature ejaculation.

I briefly tear my gaze away from Abby to peek at Major and Wade, so I can see the judgment on their faces, but it's not there.

In fact, they both mirror my own obvious desperation.

Normally, I have much more control over my initial instincts and the physical reaction of my currently unruly dick. But between the shock of seeing Abby this morning, three weeks after that mind-blowing kiss—and thinking about her pretty much everyday since—along with what happened with Wade in his room earlier, I'm riding a high I can't describe.

I need to get to know her better and I need the opportunity to challenge Wade. This also allows for the chance to give Major a bit of a show, which is right up his alley.

Attempting to relax my tense posture, I lean forward, grabbing another slice of orange, this time feeding myself as nonchalantly as I can and shrug.

"I mean, it could be fun. And everyone can have a skip," I say with more confidence than I feel, being how badly I want to play. "In fact, I don't need one so I'll donate my skip, it'll be like a free pass for anyone to use." I wiggle my eyebrows at Abby but it's Wade I think will need it.

Then Wade throws a total wrench in my cool demeanor with his response. "Sounds fun," he says with only a slight undertone of sarcasm.

He doesn't make eye contact with anyone as he reorganizes the fruit platter that doesn't need it. His usual broodiness is there but he would have referred to me as an idiot and rolled his eyes if he didn't want to play.

Playing it so fucking cool I actually impress myself and say, "Sweet," then glance over at Major. "How about you?" I ask him.

Also, in his natural state, he appraises Abby like he needs an okay from her to respond with his answer.

"I've never played," admits Major and all of our jaws drop. "Don't get me wrong, I know the rules—I get the gist, I've just never played."

"It's easy. Truth or Dare?" Abby holds her hands out, palms up like she's weighing the options. "And there's always double dare." She wiggles her eyebrows playfully with an adorable smile.

Major gives me a knowing glance because if anyone is going to do that, it's me. He sits back and passes a look by all of us, then finally turns his gaze to Abby. "If you're in, I'm in."

Abby reaches into the side pocket of her leggings and pulls out her phone.

"Ooh," I respond, as I reach in my pocket for mine, click the side button then tap at the top of her device. A pop up appears asking if I'd like to share my information. Tapping the button, yes, then craning my neck as I reach to tap *accept and share* on hers.

My phone vibrates and I add her details as a contact, quickly creating a group chat with all of us. I type out, *hey pretty girl*, hit send, then slide my phone back in my pocket.

I see the top banner pop down over the top of her screen, indicating she got the message. Her lips turn up in an adorable little smirk that she tries to hide and god, I hope I get to kiss those lips again.

She swipes the message away, glancing at the digital time display then responds with ease, "I have about an hour until I need to leave." She smiles, sliding it back into her pocket. "So, let's play."

"Yesssssss." I fistpump myself, ignoring her *'leaving in an hour'* comment.

Major leans forward, placing his glasses on the table and says, "Ladies first."

CHAPTER 13
IS THERE SUCH A THING AS A TRUTH OR DARE RATING SYSTEM?

ABBY

My eyes widen with both surprise and excitement as Major leans back in his chair. *"Ladies first."*

Geez, no pressure or anything. Doesn't he know the Pisces in me is horrible at making decisions?

Where do I start? There are so many questions I want to ask all of them. Some are completely appropriate, others not so much. I shouldn't dive straight in asking the dirty questions that have been running through my mind, but it's hard to keep my thoughts in the PG-13 direction and not dive face first into the TV-MA arena.

I glance at Major, whose gaze has been trained on me pretty much since we sat down. The interesting thing about it is, it doesn't make me feel uncomfortable or weird. It makes me feel protected, desired even.

I can't imagine someone like him taking an interest in someone like me. He's stoic and charming. His broad shoulders and lean waist sit perfectly above his strong legs and even the way he sits in a chair is silently commanding submission in a way I've never felt.

His bright eyes are kind, but there's a fire behind them I can't describe. They're laced with years of experience that match the salt and peppering at his temples and beard but his youthful glowing skin makes him seem young and playful.

I hum out loud, debating who to challenge first, as I tap my chin. "Major." His lips part slightly in surprise that I'm picking him first.

"Abby." His reply sounds like velvet to my ears, seductive yet curious.

"Truth or Dare?" I ask, lifting my eyebrows playfully.

"Truth," he responds with a confidence I envy.

"When and where was the first time you had sex?"

He doesn't even take a second to think about the question before he responds.

"Back of my dad's station wagon, prom night." He leans forward grabbing a small cluster of grapes, then leans back. "I was seventeen, she knew I was a virgin and that I was leaving for the Coast Guard after graduation, so it was like last chance, pity sex. We had no room to move, half our clothes were still on and it was way too quick." He shrugs.

"I hope your dad wasn't in the front seat," Jasper replies, and Major throws a grape at him.

"You guys throw a lot of things at each other." I giggle, stating the obvious playfulness between them all.

"He usually deserves it," Major replies. "No one's first time is good."

"Mine was," Jasper bites back quickly, as he picks up the fruit and tosses it back at Major.

"How so?" Wade asks.

Jasper is stunned as he glances over at Wade. I think he's shocked that Wade broke his silence inquiring about it.

He pauses for a moment, presses his hands into the couch cushions as he leans back and gets more comfortable.

"I was watching a movie with my best friend and his girlfriend, they started messing around under the blankets. I knew it was happening but didn't say anything." Major shifts in his seat and I lean forward with extreme curiosity. "About halfway through the movie, she straddled his lap and they started to make-out, like a heavy no holds barred make-out session. It was…hot. All of a sudden, she reached her hand out, grabbed my shirt, and pulled me in for a kiss too. Then told me she wanted to see me kiss him, my best friend. We sort of just looked at each other, pausing for a moment, but Lucy placed her hands behind our heads and just guided us together. It was the first time I ever kissed a guy and I knew instantly. Kissing a guy felt the same as kissing a girl. The same butterflies, the rush, the need. It was all there, and I loved the feeling of both." He shrugs and glances at me. "Everything sort of escalated from there." His gorgeous smile is laced with a tad bit of shyness, as he looks around the table at all of us.

My hand mindlessly flaps twice in front of me attempting to secretly fan myself, as I expel the breath I was holding during his story. I feel like my body is on fire and my cheeks are probably the same color as the fire truck that sits in the garage.

It's my turn to shift in my seat, as I attempt to gain some control and retract the tingling sensation between my legs.

My god. That was…wow.

I'm confused by my reaction. Whenever I've thought of sex or sexual pleasures, it's always been with a guy and a girl. I never expected to be so turned on by hearing a story of a guy with another man but I feel feral in ways I can't describe.

I clear my throat. "Whose turn is it?" I ask.

"Jasper." Major's voice is husky but calm. "Truth or Dare?"

Jasper's smile widens in slow motion as he looks back at Major with a glint in his eye. Like he's challenging Major himself.

"Dare. Always, dare."

CHAPTER 14
EXPECT THE UNEXPECTED AND BRING SNACKS. WE'VE GOT A FRONT ROW VIEW TO ORGASMVILLE

WADE

I need to get out of here. I need to leave.

The sexual tension between everyone right now is thick and heavy, just like my unmanageable cock that strains against my pants.

I palm my face to train my expression. Embarrassed that everyone will see right through how much Jasper's story almost threw me over the edge. I'd consider streaking through the streets naked in the middle of day to get a front row seat to watch how that all unfolded.

Okay, I probably wouldn't, but the fact that I considered it is enough for me to know how badly I want to witness it…*be* a part of it.

I grip the wooden handle of the chair, my knuckles blanching white with the tightness of the grip as my emotions battle each other. It flows through me like lava, and I'm both aroused and pissed off.

I hate that Jasper's had another man before. Which is stupid to feel that way. He's had men and women. But there's something about knowing that Jasper has pleasured another man, just like he so easily pleasured me, has me seeing red.

Major side-eyes me then looks back at Jasper, as he taunts us with his dare.

You could hear a star falling with how silent the space around us is.

"I dare you to kiss Abby."

Abby's breath hitches as her gaze snaps to Majors then flickers over to mine. I appraise her to see her reaction because I don't want her to feel uncomfortable, but based on her flushed cheeks and that nibble at the corner of her mouth, she looks far from it.

A smile spreads across Jasper's face as he looks directly at me, one eyebrow raises to the top of his forehead, as if to remind me of his *I'm going to kiss her* comment from earlier today.

Too late, I kissed her first, sucker.

I smile back mirroring his expression, challenging him to complete his dare.

Jasper leans forward, picking up a mint leaf I placed on the fruit platter and places it on his tongue before chewing then swallows as he turns toward Abby. "So what do you say? You good with that, pumpkin?"

Her eyes flicker over to mine again with a questionable look behind them, as if she's checking to see if I'm upset. But she won't find that. She'll only find the same need and yearning that matches hers.

Leaning forward, I place my elbows on my thighs because everything in me is engaged in her, in them. I smother a smile but not enough to hide the inevitable smirk as we pass each other knowing glances.

Her lips squeeze together, forming a tight line as she looks back at Jasper and softly nods.

"Thank fucking god." Jasper pushes himself forward, pressing one knee into the couch as he hovers over her. He cups her cheeks with both hands, using a gentle grip to pull her toward him.

She sits taller, meeting him halfway, as he tenderly presses his lips to hers.

His eyes squeeze tight, like this kiss is as painful as it is pleasurable.

And it's as if they can read each other without words, because their lips part naturally and their tongues clash together perfectly in line with each other. A synchronized moan passes between them as their kiss morphs from a soft, desperate one to a passionate, more demanding one.

Major and I match our movement as we lean closer, needing to take in more of the view, needing to get closer to feel the same sensation they are.

It's a kiss. People kiss all the time. But this…this could suck the soul from your body and bring you back from the dead simultaneously.

It's the same sensation I had when we had our kiss, like I could feel the half of my heart that I thought was dead come back to life.

Jaspers hand trails to the nape of her neck, allowing him to pull her even deeper and their bodies are now flush together. His hips push forward as she circles hers and a guttural groan comes from somewhere in the middle of Jasper's body.

He pulls back, hissing. His gaze urgently bounces between her eyes and mouth, then he pulls her back into him, desperate for more.

"Mmmm," Abby moans, and the sound goes straight to my cock. Major shifts back in his seat and clears his throat loudly, attempting to remind them of where they are.

Jasper blindly points at him without stopping the kiss, then says, "Don't do that. Don't play the cut-off music."

Abby giggles and tosses her head back. Jasper groans again, this time it sounds happy and playful. Like he just took a bite of a Michelin star dessert and it was the best thing he's ever eaten. His arms are still wrapped around her as he squeezes her like he never wants to let her go. He nuzzles into her neck, whispering something I can't hear, then finally loosens his embrace enough for them to pull back and gaze into each other's eyes.

Jasper doesn't waste any time. "Truth or Dare?"

A lengthy pause passes between them. Abby purses her lips and blows out a silent breath, sneaking glances at both me and Major.

"God, I'm going to regret this." She shakes her head as she softly closes her eyes and huffs out a breath. "Dare."

Jasper's face splits into another mile wide smile. His neck swivels slightly in my direction, side-eying me, then his gaze shifts back on Abby.

"I dare you to kiss Wade."

What?

Not that Jasper is a particularly selfish person but I fully expected him to dare her to do something more to him, not to someone else.

I wear the surprised look on my face as easily as I wear my typical scowl of displeasure, especially when it comes to Jasper. He doesn't know we kissed earlier, and sure it's just a kiss and we're all adults but I hate the thought of Abby potentially being uncomfortable. I think he's intentionally going out of his way to make things awkward and that pisses me off because it's involving Abby.

I go to open my mouth to scold Jasper but I'm cut off by Abby's reply. "Well, that's an easy one." She gives me a knowing glance and my eyebrows hit my hairline, surprised by another shocking response. My eyes bounce between the two of them, almost as if prepared for a joke but it doesn't come.

She pushes herself off the couch into a standing position, straightening out the oversized sweater that hangs over her shoulder. Her outfit is casual but she somehow makes it look elegant and so goddamn sexy.

A portion of her sun kissed skin is peeking out from the top of where the sleeve of her sweater drapes passed her shoulder. The strap of her black top is lacy and I can't tell if it's a bra or a tank top and whether or not there's less or more underneath. All I know is the fabric is thin allowing her pert nipples to shadow through the front, stirring my hard cock even further.

I sit back in my chair, unsure of what to do with myself as she takes a step in my direction. She wastes no time swinging one leg over my body, placing herself on my lap, straddling me. My hands naturally cup around her full, lush hips, that fit like a glove over my own.

Her face is inches from mine. The same alluring scent that floated around me in my room while we built the Lego together engulfs me again, pulling me further into heaven. It smells like citrus and sugar and I can't seem to get enough of it.

"Can I kiss you again, sweetheart?"

"I kissed *you* last time."

"Ehhhh," I squeak out, bouncing my head back and forth, "that's subjective." I smile looking at her, then look past her shoulder and my gaze meets Jaspers. It's not often I can get a rise out of him but the way his jaw is slacked tells me I just did.

"Say, what?" Jasper replies. "You guys already kissed?"

Abby tosses her head back with a laugh, exposing even more of her gorgeous neckline. I lean closer, pressing my nose into her nook, taking even more of her in. Her hands that were loosely placed on my shoulders move to cup my jaw, and her body rolls into mine, as my hot breath trails over her soft skin.

When I glance back up and she's looking down at me, we're face to face with matching reflections of pure desire.

Craning my neck forward, I press my lips to hers, swallowing the moan from her mouth. I run the tip of my tongue over her bottom lip before pulling her further into me as our mouths collide and a shiver rolls through my entire body with just a kiss and I wonder how my body would respond to her if we were completely naked, my tongue caressing every inch of her gorgeous body.

I imagine her straddling me, like she is now, wearing nothing but her addictive smile and the long strands of her silky hair draping over her sun-kissed skin, with a look of ecstasy on her face as she rocks her hips over mine. I close my eyes and visualize Jasper hovering over us telling her what a good girl she is and how sexy she looks riding my cock, while Major watches in a corner.

"Umpf," I groan uncontrollably at the image. My hips buck and my cock twitches, pulling another moan from Abby.

I didn't realize how close I had pulled her into me and how much our bodies were spiraling together until I opened my eyes. I peer over at Major whose body is frozen and rigid as he sits stoic in his chair. I can't be sure he's even breathing.

Jasper chipmunks his cheeks, blowing out a long breath. "Well, that was…nice." The last word comes out in a questionable tone and is a completely inaccurate description of what that was.

Weather is *nice*. People are *nice*.

That was super-fucking-natural.

"Mmmm." Abby moans, her teeth pull in that bottom lip I can't seem to get enough of as her eyes open softly. "Your turn."

My brows furrow in confusion for a brief moment, until I remember that we're playing a game.

"Oh, right." I glance back at the guys, who are more composed than me in a way I'm jealous of. Abby attempts to push herself off me, but I tighten my grip on her hips.

Not only do I not want her to leave, the obvious tent in my pants would be a complete embarrassment considering how put together Jasper was when he kissed Abby.

She settles into me, wrapping her arms around my neck like

it's the most natural thing, "Truth or Dare?" she asks with a tight lipped smile.

I glance around the room again, taking in the comfort of the space I live in more than half my life, with the guys that I feel the most comfortable with. Sure, Jasper and I have always fought, bickered back and forth, but he's always been reliable and loyal.

It isn't his fault that I've had an attraction to him I could never figure out. I've always erred on the side of caution with everything in my life, especially after having Lily.

But now is not the time for that.

"Double Dare."

CHAPTER 15
JUST CALL ME JOHNNY 5, BECAUSE I'M SHORT CIRCUITING

JASPER

I'm speechless for the second time tonight.

That's a lie. I've been battling with my mind-mouth connection all goddamn day. Typically, I have zero filter saying whatever comes to mind, but today every time anyone says anything even partially related to sex, I have a full body malfunction.

Wade said double dare.

I've never known this man to take a risk on anything in his life. He's cautious to a fault and annoyingly strategic in every-thing he does.

So, double dare, yeah…I'm fucking speechless. And by the look on Major's face, he's just as stunned as I am.

At least I know I'm not hearing things.

My mind can't help but spiral, thinking of all the things I could do if he would have said that to me. I would have challenged him for a repeat of what happened in his room. No, I would force him to tell me what he was visualizing when he said *that's it, both of you take my cock,* so I could recreate that scenario for him in real life.

"Oh." Abby's surprise mirrors all of ours as she looks over at Major, then peers over her shoulder back at me.

I wish I knew her better so I could predict what's going to happen next. She must know that all of us are open to whatever might happen next, and she has every single man in this room at her mercy. But, I have no idea if she's a risk taker or a play-it-safe kind of girl, and the unknown is killing me.

And because my brain isn't functioning with basic vocabulary today, I silently respond with a tight-lipped smile and an idiotic look on my face.

She huffs out a light chuckle before biting the corner of her lip, then turns her gaze back to Wade.

"Are you sure? No take backs," she says playfully.

Wade chews on the inside of his cheek, his eyes shift briefly in my direction before locking back on hers. He contemplates for less time than I expect him to before nodding. "Oh, I'm sure, sweetheart."

CHAPTER 16
THIS IS DEFINITELY NOT SCATTERGORIES

MAJOR

What in the everloving hell is happening?

We were supposed to be playing Scrabble or Monopoly or some other boring archaic board game, not the Truth or Dare kissing game with the most gorgeous woman I've ever laid my eyes on with three times more testosterone than necessary.

God, I'm too old for this shit.

Of course, I'm saying that to myself but I'm enjoying every minute of watching this unfold.

The sexual tension between Wade and Jasper has always been there. I've felt it even if those two masked it in the form of hatred. But now, adding Abby into the mix, well that's like adding fuel to an already burning inferno.

And I have no idea how to respond to the guys right now. Because Truth or Dare Wade is nothing like the man I normally know. It's like he's hijacked the confidence that Jasper usually has, leaving Jasper confused and distorted.

My gaze trails over to the lost man as he sits on the couch opposite Wade and Abby. His shaggy blonde hair is disheveled from when Abby kissed him, gripping onto his scalp like she never wanted to let him go. But also, because he keeps running his hand through it, as if that's a nervous tick I've never seen him have.

He's beyond flustered, that much is obvious. I can't say I don't relate.

Watching Abby all day as she recorded videos of herself, and all of us, for her social media account was surprisingly a tease I didn't know I would enjoy. But seeing her interact with the guys, pulling out sides of them I've never seen before and now these two mind-blowing, life-altering kisses. Yeah, I feel like a giddy teenager and a born-again man going through sexual rebirth at the same time.

I'm battling with myself to remain calm and maintain the control that I typically have in most situations. But let's face it, none of this is like any situation I would have imagined myself in. Especially with a woman, almost twenty years younger than me and with both of the guys I lean on the most professionally.

This is a bad idea. This is a really bad idea.

I repeat that over and over to myself, but it doesn't seem to help my resolve when I lean back in my chair, signaling to the group that I'm happy and comfortable in the seat I'm in watching, observing.

Abby glances over to me, her eyes trail my relaxed form and a sheepish smile appears over that gorgeous face. Her brows tick up and I wonder if she's thinking exactly what I was trying to tell her during our conversation in the garage earlier.

These guys may look like they want to kill each other, but given the chance, they'd fall to their knees for each other.

Abby returns that same knowing look before turning back to Wade.

His chest rises as dramatically as it falls. As cool as he appears I know he's balancing on a tightrope in his head. The one that Abby currently has full control over.

"Wade…" Everyone stops breathing. "I double dare you," she leans in closer to him, her eyes bouncing between his eyes and lips, "to recreate Jasper's first kiss…with Jasper."

"Oh shit." Jasper chokes on his own saliva as he whispers the words.

Wade's breathing picks up, a crease forms between his eyes as he takes in Abby's words. His fists clench around her hips, as if trying to reel himself in, probably unsure if he wants to freak out and run out of the room or lift his chin and take on her challenge.

I clear my throat, not because I'm trying to push him but because I forgot I stopped breathing. It's the same state everyone is currently in.

Wade side-eyes in my direction, glances over at Jasper then his eyes rise up to meet Abby's, who's still straddling his lap. Their eyes lock on each other and it's as if you can hear them click in place.

Keeping his eyes locked on hers, he finally says, "Jasper, get over here."

CHAPTER 17
EXCUSE ME WHILE I CLAIM TEMPORARY INSANITY

WADE

I swallow thickly attempting to coat my dry throat with something other than sandpaper and nerves.

I have no idea where my confidence is coming from…actually, I do. It's coming from the gorgeous woman currently sitting on my lap, looking down at me with nothing but admiration behind them and a satisfied smirk on those plump lips of hers.

Lips I lost myself in twice today.

A sound rustles behind her but I ignore it, knowing it's Jasper slowly inching his way toward us. Instead of looking at him, I keep my eyes locked on Abby, drawing the assurance I need from her.

Her long, dark hair drapes over her shoulders, covering the top half of her body almost entirely. I want to cup her face and tuck the thick curtain behind her ear but I almost feel as if it's blocking us from the outside world. The private serenity gives me the courage I've been searching for.

How is it that she's known all of us for only a few short hours, yet it feels like a lifetime she's been part of our circle? The comfort she brings is undeniable. And I know if I asked the guys the same question, they wouldn't have a reasonable explanation either.

Jasper appears in my periphery, he's pulling his normally shaggy hair into his signature manbun and I love when he wears it that way.

I'd never admit that to him though.

He kneels down beside the chair that Abby is straddling me in, but still I keep my eyes on her. I don't trust how my body or mind will respond when I see him sitting so close to me. I already feel him when he's close, like my entire body is a Jasper locating radar and my body starts to tingle whenever he is near.

Abby gives me a comforting smile and I mirror it back before closing my eyes and sucking in a deep breath. As I reopen them, they shift over in the direction of the man that I've trained myself to despise, knowing if I allowed myself to open up to him, I would lose all sense of myself. But as our eyes connect, it's the first time I don't care about the normalcy of my life or fight with myself to stop the natural response my body has to him.

I just want him to kiss me like his life fucking depends on it.

I want him to claim me, like he claimed his best friend.

Abby begins to lift off me but I tense my hands tighter around her hips. I need her to stay. Not only is she a comfort blanket that is covering up my massive erection, but she's protecting me from full exposure to Jasper. Which is something I know I need.

She stops pulling away from me and sits back down, placing one hand on my shoulder while her other hand cups my jaw, forcing my gaze back to hers. Without any other warning, she leans into me kissing me again, and this time knowing it's because she really wants to and not because it's a dare, makes my stomach flip and my heart beats so hard I can feel it in every corner of my body.

She releases her hand from my jaw and I hate how the cold

air hits my skin so I pull her flush against my body, needing more of the comfort she brings. Her other hand moves up the column of my neck, gripping the hair at my nape. It's gentle but commanding and when her lips leave mine, I know exactly what to expect when I open my eyes.

But that still doesn't prepare me against the foreign sensation of seeing Jasper's face just inches from mine as she guides us closer together.

His tongue darts out, wetting his bottom lip and the feral look in his eyes is a complete reflection of my own.

Our bodies slowly eat up the space between us as my eyes bounce between his lips and eyes. The incessant flipping that was happening in my stomach earlier is now replaced with an amusement park of roller coasters, going nonstop and uncontrollably faster, as Jasper slowly leans closer to me.

With his hair pulled back, it shows off the sharp features of his chiseled jawline and high cheekbones. His face is never clean shaven and almost always has the short stubble that looks like he forgot to shave, even though I know he does because the short blonde shavings are always left in our shared bathroom sink, and I always find myself cleaning them up for him.

The darkness of his pupils are invading the crystal green color of his irises, giving him the look of a wild animal instead of the playful Jasper I'm used to seeing. They're usually light and perky. But now, they're dark and needy, laced with a trepidation I'm not used to.

And I realize for the first time since I've known Jasper, he's nervous. His breath is labored with heavy short breaths and his eyes dance around every corner of my face as if committing it to memory.

I lean closer, as if to comfort him but I feel resistance as Jasper pulls back and my heart drops, fearing rejection. His head moves slowly from side to side, like he's talking himself out of it, then he sucks in a commanding breath, whispering, "I've wanted to do this for so fucking long," then he crashes his lips against mine.

An unruly, guttural moan escapes my body and I wish I could take it back, until I hear Jasper release one of his own. My lips part further as his tongue dips into my mouth and the sensation is so unbelievably foreign yet so fucking incredible, I can't help but push my hips into Abby, needing more, begging for more.

A mix of the cedar, sage scent I know so well of him engulfs me again today and I flashback to our discretions in the dark in my room earlier and my cock twitches at the thought.

Abby rolls her hips into mine and I have to grip her hips to hold her in place because I will absolutely lose all control if Jasper keeps kissing me like this while she does that.

A muffled, "fuck," comes out between my lips. I never want this to stop.

The sensation I have can only be described as Jasper said. It's the same feeling I get when kissing a woman. The same powerful desire, the stomach flip. All of it is there.

My eyebrows pinch together, as if confused by the thought. I break our kiss and dip my chin to my chest, peering down to avoid eye contact.

I shouldn't feel ashamed of these feelings but I do. I shouldn't like any of this. I internally scold myself, blinking quickly trying to pull myself together.

Jasper's fingers grip my face, forcing me to look at him and I hate that he's doing that. He's not giving me a chance to work through my puzzled thoughts, the ones making me pull away from both Abby and Jasper. And I don't want to allow myself to look over at Major to try and figure out what he might be thinking.

But when my eyes connect with Jaspers, he's still feral and needy. They're just laced with a concern I can relate to, and I see him trying to understand that I need time. But because it's Jasper, he doesn't give it to me.

"Don't you do that." He shakes his head at me. "I know what you're thinking and you need to knock it the fuck off, right now."

His eyes flicker between my eyes and lips again and I see how much restraint he has with himself. This time it isn't a dare that's pulling us together, it's his choice, and maybe mine too. I can't tell if I'm leaning into him too, or if I'm frozen in time, afraid to do anything to take me out of this moment.

A loud buzzing suddenly takes over the space around us and something begins to vibrate on my leg. Abby's breath hitches as she startles and now my brows really pinch in confusion. I look down between where Abby is straddling me and where the vibration is coming from and I see Jasper do the same. Then a ringing sound echoes through the room and she jumps, patting the back of her pocket as she reaches for her phone.

"I'm so sorry. I have to take this," she says, answering her phone, then whips one leg over my body and stands walking away from Jasper and I, leaving him kneeling on the ground next to my chair in an awkward ending to that mind-blowing kiss.

I rip my eyes away from Jasper, afraid of what I'll feel and see when I look at him. Without the *Abby wall of infinite protection* I feel exposed, vulnerable, and I'm not sure I can do anything without her here.

I avoid him by glancing over to Major, wondering what he's thinking and it's clear he's just as confused as I am. But where my expression is laced with confusion and fear, his is different.

And I realize when he side-eyes a glance at Abby as she walks toward the front entrance, that she's the one causing his confusion, not from what Jasper and I just did. His expression fades quickly, as most do with Major, then he presses into his heels, standing to his full height.

"It's about fucking time you two did that," he says, as he passes by us to follow Abby.

CHAPTER 18

SOME TRADITIONS CAN USE AN UPGRADE, IN THE FORM OF THREE TEMPTING FIREMEN

ABBY

"Cami, it's our tradition," I remind her, a little begging in my tone.

"I know, I'm sorry, but my sister can really use the help today." Her response is a bit clipped and I don't know if I'm reading more into it or if I'm just being extra sensitive.

"I can help," I say as more of a question than a statement, further clarifying my needy tone.

I really don't want to spend Christmas Eve alone. I already spend Christmas day by myself and have for the last two years.

I have over a million followers on my social media accounts but no one to spend a holiday with. It's funny, the perception that people may have of someone based on what's in black and white on the internet.

"The recital is for family only. I'm sorry Abby. I'll make it up to you." Her words aren't mean but they hurt all the same, because her statement just reminds me; I'm no one's family.

"Yeah, no, I understand. I'll just binge out on that new Netflix show or start a new book. If you finish early though, call me, okay?" I say with a little too much pleading in the tone.

"Sure thing, of course. Have fun and I'll call you later." She disconnects quickly and I stand frozen in disappointment.

I know it shouldn't bother me as much as it does, but I can't help feeling let down. I know she's not responsible to keep me company but she knows how affected I am by this holiday.

I never used to hate this time of year, in fact I used to love it. Christmas was my favorite time of the year and all of the holiday parties, Christmas music, and joyful events that led up to it was something I looked forward to. But both of my parents died in the month of December, now making this my most dreaded time of the year.

I try to pack it full of things to do, to keep my mind off all the bad stuff. Sometimes it helps. But most of the time I'm just scrambling, trying to keep my mind and body busy.

Maybe that's why I created the platform I have now. I was seeking acceptance, seeking friendships. Sadly, it's only made everything more difficult, because people no longer see you as a person, they see you as a resource to get more followers or gain popularity.

I'm sure some of them are genuine and some amazing relationships can come out of it. But after what Sam did to me, I have a hard time trusting that someone doesn't have an ulterior motive.

Glancing out the blacked out window at the front of the fire station I realize just how out of the place I am. I gaze at a smudge on the window and allow my vision to blur around me. I need to do what I always do and ignore the loneliness that surrounds this holiday.

Until Cami called, it actually hadn't crossed my mind. I guess I looked forward to meeting her for our Christmas Eve movie marathon and didn't focus on knowing I would wake up alone on Christmas day yet again this year.

The distraction of three very attractive firefighters has helped too. And not only are they mind-blowingly sexy, but they're all fun and easy to get along with.

It's interesting what the power of personal connections do. Jasper, Wade, and Major's company have made me live completely in the moment today. I usually have to work so much harder to divert the thoughts of being alone and feeling unloved.

These guys have easily put themselves at the forefront of my mind and nothing has felt forced or fake. It actually feels like we've known each other for longer than we have.

I've had time with each of them, individually and together and, well…the together part…that was explosive.

Watching Jasper and Wade kiss mere inches from me while Major shadowed us was the most sensual thing I've ever been a part of. It might have looked like just a simple kiss on the outside, but the unrelenting passion they had for each other in that moment rivaled any kiss I've ever physically experienced.

Cami's call couldn't have had worse timing and I probably shouldn't have answered, but I figured she was leaving to meet me at my house and I didn't want to let her down. I should have just let it go to voicemail so I could see where that kiss would lead to.

I'm ashamed to admit how much more I want to see of them —all of us—together, but now it'll just be awkward walking back in there expecting to pick up right where we left off. Plus, I glance at my watch, it's time for me to go. I've been here far too long and ultimately these guys are probably just trying to be nice and humor me with all the things I brought them.

"Hey, everything okay?" I startle, whiplashing my neck in Major's direction.

His stoic, strong form is standing in the archway that connects the front office to the garage and I'm curious as to how long he's been there. His keen sense of awareness is on full display as his eyes lock on mine like he's trying to read all the thoughts running through my head.

"Oh yeah, everything is great," I lie through my teeth, "I should just head out soon to meet my friend." There I go, lying again.

"The friend that just canceled on you?" Oh, great. So, not only did he overhear my conversation, but he heard how sad and desperate I sounded. "Was that a *guy* friend or a *girl* friend.?" he asks with a smidge of shyness behind his tone.

My shoulders deflate as they drop to my sides. I know he heard enough that I can't keep up a lie, even though I'd rather ignore this conversation.

"My friend, Cami. She usually keeps me company on Christmas Eve but something came up," I state factually.

"What do you mean keeps you company?" he asks, as he takes a step toward me, lining himself up in front of me.

"It's a tradition we started quite a few years back. She comes over for Christmas Eve and we binge out on random movies and eat junk food all night long. It's been a tradition since my dad passed. I didn't realize how much I needed it until I lost my mother a couple years ago." I glance up at him with a tight-lipped smile. I'm not looking for any type of pity, but I do want him to know why I'm feeling disappointed.

He nods slowly as he takes in the information. He places his hand on my shoulder, caressing my arm, as his fingers slowly trail down to my hand. The pads of his fingers massage the column between my own, my mouth naturally forms an O shape and my breath stalls at how sensitive and sensual the motion is.

Like who knew something so simple would feel so unbeliev-able. But here I am, getting a finger massage like I've been deprived of touch my entire life.

His other hand cups my slacked jaw, forcing me to tip my chin up toward him.

"I hate to break the bad news to your friend, but you have three very interested men that would love to give you a new Christmas Eve tradition."

"Oh yeah?" I can't help but smile.

He nods, with a lopsided smirk and squint in his eye. The slight graying at his temples contradicts his cute, boyish demeanor.

He's still massaging my fingers as he leans down, his eyes bouncing between my eyes and lips. A scent, so distinctly him, invades the space around me, engulfing me. It's sweet and spicy and different from the woodsy sage scent that Jasper has or the sweet mint flavor of Wade's lips.

"I'm going to kiss you now. Then we're going to walk back in there and figure out what other traditions we can make tonight."

How my smile can get any bigger I have no idea. He doesn't give it anymore time though. He presses his lips to mine and I purse back, cupping both my hands around his face at the same time our tongues meet. It's just as explosive as my kiss with Jasper, just like the one with Wade, and I have no idea how any of this makes sense.

Each of these men are so different, so unique in their own way. Yet, the intimacy I experience with each of them is far beyond anything I could imagine.

Major moans and pulls back, his fingers stop massaging mine and his hand folds into my palm as if he needs to hold me in place.

"I knew before, but now I really know," he says.

"Know what?" I ask.

"The reason why the guys are so obsessed and never want you to leave."

I roll my eyes and huff out a shy giggle as I shake my head. We've had fun but that's all this is... *just* fun. I'll be leaving soon and this whole experience will be a passing thought for all of them.

"I'm serious, princess." He steps away, not letting go of my hand as he leads me back through the archway. "We're not letting you get away that easily."

CHAPTER 19
I AM THE SELF-PROCLAIMED MASTER OF GOOD IDEAS

JASPER

"Do you think he's talking to her?" Wade asks as he stares out the open doorway into the garage.

"Yes," I chuckle, "I'm sure he is."

"I mean trying to talk her into staying longer?" He glances over at me and it's the first time I've ever seen his eyes look so vulnerable.

Normally Wade is curt and short with me. But the way he's looking at me now, with both a feral need and a desperate longing for Abby to stay, is a sight that would literally put me to my knees.

I'll never get over how much I want him now that I've had a taste of him. And somehow, the sweet citrus flavor from Abby's lips mixed with that tantalizing mint spice that follows Wade around like a lost puppy has created an addictive combination that I couldn't be more obsessed with.

"If anyone can, it's him," I state factually, because Major is incredibly persuasive and it's not often he doesn't find a way to make things happen. Especially when it comes to things that revolve around the people he cares about.

Even though I know Major wants this—probably just as much as we do—he wouldn't act on it for himself alone. He's selfless that way. And he'll find too many excuses to put her out of his league if it were solely for his benefit. But, I see how she affects him, just as badly as she affects me and Wade. There is something happening between all of us and if we don't explore this I'll regret it for the rest of my life.

"I have an idea." Wade's wide, curious eyes trail my movement as I walk through the doorway and into the garage.

Turning the corner, I pass the line of wall mounted storage lockers until I find mine. Reaching into my cubby, I grab the yellow corded rope that's tied neatly into an infinity loop and then dig into my bag pulling out a clean bandana. Sometimes I'll wear one under my helmet to help manage the sweat from the heat we have to endure, but this will be useful for a whole other reason tonight.

I run my hand over our turnout gear and glance between the rope, bandana, and fire truck smiling to myself because I have the best fucking idea. I know Major will massively frown upon it, but I'm not sure I care enough to worry about what he thinks at this point.

He's just as invested as we are and sometimes he needs a little push.

Wade too.

I rummage through my bag, I'm not exactly sure what I'm looking for, just something that might contribute more to my plan and freeze when I see the shirt I wore at the Farmers Market the day I met Abby.

It's a basic white tee, but dons the words, *Lettuce Turnip the Beet* down the middle. I remember she asked if it was because I like music or vegetables, but now it carries a whole new meaning.

I tuck the bandana in my back pocket and hold onto the shirt and rope as I walk back to our rec room where a majority of our time has been spent today, which isn't uncommon, but I'm not sure I'll be able to easily erase the memories from tonight out of it.

I've always had an unhealthy obsession when it comes to Wade. Normally I would ignore unrequited feelings and move on knowing someone wasn't interested. But with Wade, I couldn't. I can't.

That same feeling washed over me the moment Abby and I kissed at the Farmers Market and I remember how desperate I was for her to stay. I was praying to every God in the universe that she would come back to our booth. When she never came back and I was called into the station, I left feeling like I missed a once-in-a-lifetime opportunity.

And I was right, because for the short time she's been here, Major is less rigid and more open and Wade, well fuck, Wade is night and day a completely different man.

Except at this moment, when I turn the corner and he sees an article of clothing in one hand and a rope in my other.

One eyebrow shoots up and that questioning glare that he would always pin me with is back. There's less animosity behind it than before but a part of me hopes I still bring out a bit of that exasperated side of him I love so much.

"I would ask you what you're up to, but I probably don't want to know the answer." He squints at me, as if he is in pain preparing for a verbal lashing.

"Then I won't tell you and you can be just as surprised as Abby and Major."

"Oh, no." He shakes his head as he stands and makes his way over to me with that scowl I crave. God, he's delicious. "Now you have to tell me so I can talk you out of it before you get us both fired."

I ignore him as I tuck the rope in my back pocket, opposite the bandana and set the T-shirt down on the island. Grabbing a few pieces of paper, scissors, a sharpie, and a couple safety pins from the junk drawer I begin creating my visionary masterpiece.

I cut the paper to fit over the letters, the sizing isn't exact but it'll do. Then, with the sharpie, I write the letter H on one and the letter A on another, pinning it over the B and the E.

I spread the shirt, face up with the words on display over the countertop. Wade curls his head to the side as he appraises it with a pinch in his brow. Probably from confusion as to what I'm doing and judging my artistry skills which I'm only partially offended by.

"Lettuce turnip the heat," he reads out loud. "That doesn't make any sense."

I look at him sideways. "Let us…turn up…the *heat*." I flail my arms between the two of us and around the room. "We're firefighters." Duh.

"Okay, yeah but what are we going to do? Light her on fire?"

"Hopefully." I wiggle my eyebrows at him as I pull the bandana, aka blindfold, and rope from my pocket, dropping them strategically on each side of the shirt.

"No. No, no, no," Wade repeats multiple times, as he shakes his head, like I didn't hear the first four no's. Then grabs the rope, looking around like he intends to hide it.

"Hey." I snatch it back but his grip is like fucking super glue and now we're pulling it back and forth, neither one of us wanting to let go.

"I don't even fully know what you're planning to do with all of this but I don't like it."

"You will if you heard me out."

"I guarantee you, I won't."

"It's a good idea."

"It's really not."

"How would you know?"

"How would he know what?" Major says and we both turn to

face the doorway. Major and Abby stand, hand in hand, wide-eyed as the look between me and Wade.

I glance back at Wade giving him a shit eating grin and he silently eyes me with a contemplative look mixed with '*please don't* and *shut your fucking mouth.*' He's so damn cute when he's pissed.

"We were just discussing the next round of Truth or Dare," I reply. "Wade didn't think you guys would be up for it." I yank on the rope now that Wade loosened his grip, giving him a little smirk because I won that round of tug-of-war.

Giving it a little spin in the air, I catch it back in my hand before tossing it in Abby's direction. It flies through the room between us and lands squarely in her open hands.

Turning the rope over in her hand, she looks at it then takes a few steps in our direction, lifting her chin to see my amazing piece of artwork in my makeshift T-shirt message.

The corner of her lip lifts up, then the other, beaming into a full blown smile, and damn, she's stunning.

"Lettuce turnip the heat, huh?" she says, "And how do you intend to do that?" she asks, picking up the bandana. Her eyebrows are raised in curiosity as she peers over to me.

"Ever play Guess Who?"

CHAPTER 20
THIS IS A REALLY BAD IDEA

MAJOR

I am definitely getting fired over this.

Surprisingly, I'm less concerned about that and more curious about Abby's response. And by the looks of it, Jasper and Wade are in the same boat as I am. Breath held, unblinking.

I swallow the lump in my throat wishing it would take my nerves with it as I stare silently at Abby also wishing she would have said something by now.

Jasper looks confident and sure of himself. Wade looks like he might vomit.

Nothing more needs to be said about what playing *Guess Who* with a bandana and rope might mean. I carefully observe Abby as she runs her fingers over the tight material of the rope and soft fabric of the bandana and with how delayed her response time is, I'm thinking I need to step in and redirect this conversation elsewhere.

This is a lot. We are a lot and I want her to feel comfortable here. I don't want her to feel pressured into playing a game that puts her in a compromising position.

Albeit, a fucking sexy one.

Her blindfolded, tied with her hands behind her back as we take turns kissing her, touching her, pleasing her. My cock stirs behind my pants for the…I pause, because I've lost count how many times I felt my dick whiz to life since Abby showed up here.

It's been more today than it has been in the past month…well months. That's an embarrassing fact, but unfortunately a true one. It has been a *really* long time since my body has physically responded to any woman.

And speaking of too long, Abby still hasn't said anything. It's probably only been a few seconds but in the confines of my head it feels like hours.

I need to give her an out in case she doesn't feel like she has one.

Stepping forward, I open my mouth to begin to call this whole thing off but Abby's words surprise me yet again.

"I happen to be the undisputed, undefeated champion of Guess Who. National winner of the Guess Who championships. You guys have no idea what you're getting into."

Jasper steps toward her with that slow, sexy smile of his and a cocky expression. He holds his palm out, silently asking for the rope and bandana. She hands it to him wordlessly as they stare each other down like it's high noon on the western frontier.

And of course Jasper has to up the ante.

"Wanna bet on it?"

CHAPTER 21
BOY SCOUTS ARE PROFESSIONAL ROPE TYER'S

ABBY

I've always considered myself to be a playful, easy-going person. I do need some structure in my life, a schedule to maintain some routine, but if it's too strict or rigid, I burn out easily.

I'll still commit myself to certain things, regretting it later when I feel like it zaps the joy out of whatever it is I was supposed to do.

In the brief time I've known these guys, I've noticed there's a balance between them that they probably need in order to do the kind of work they do.

Major, being the militant one, keeping everyone on track but he probably forgets to have fun unless he's forced into it. Jasper is a complete one-eighty from Major, who probably forgets his obligations when he's having too much fun, and Wade is like a seesaw in between the two of them, going one way or the other depending on who convinces him on which direction to go.

I find myself in that predicament, as my eyes rebound back and forth between Jasper's bright, playful eyes—a notch more feral than usual—and Major's dark and serious gaze.

Major's searing stare makes me feel safe and protected while Jasper's pulls a curiosity and excitement from me that reminds me I enjoy that easy-going side of myself. The one I haven't seen much of since my parents died.

Jasper's confidence rivals that of Iron Man right now and I know, at this very moment, I am no match for this man or this game.

Not only have I never played Guess Who in my entire twenty-seven years of life, I'm actually terrible at guessing games and any type of trivia.

So betting on this, suicide. Complete and utter suicide.

"What did you have in mind?" I reply, because apparently I have a gambling addiction to these three men and I don't know how to stop.

Jasper leans into me, grazing his lips across the shell of my ear. "Do you trust me, pumpkin?"

He trails the rounded tip of the looped rope down my arm and I'm surprised at how soft it feels. Shivers run through my body, goosebumps forming over every exposed surface area and my breath stalls in my chest.

His tone is sensual and kind, but assertive and demanding all at the same time.

I nod, because I do trust him, even though he's managed to steal my breath from my body with one question.

"Good. But after everything I have planned for you, you probably shouldn't." He nips at my ear and I gasp out a moan. "Follow me." He threads his fingers through mine and leads me into the garage with Wade and Major in hurried steps behind us.

The sun is just setting, making the expansive space darker than it was earlier. There are a few deep yellow lights strategically placed above certain areas of the lockers and surrounding storage areas, creating an amber-colored ambience that feels cozy and warm considering we're pretty much in a cement garage.

Jasper walks us toward the large fire truck, the back end cargo door is open, exposing a small cubby area that holds some stacked construction cones, a metal box, and what appears to be electrical panelling tucked inside.

There's a small ladder bolted to the right side which Jasper heads straight for. Then he stops, grabs my waist, turns me around and guides me up against it.

He makes quick work unwrapping the rope as it splays open then dangles to the floor. He takes one end and expertly ties a knot around my wrist before tucking the length of it behind and through the steps of the ladder to the opposite side. The rope falls to my left side and he quickly wraps another knot around my other wrist.

My heart rate is sky high and I can feel the hard pumping of its beat over every inch of my body.

There's a brief moment where I feel thankful for the slack in the rope, since I can still move my arms. The thick, corded braid spiral rolls side-to-side over the step ladder allowing me to see-saw my arms back and forth.

That is until he places one foot on the flat metal bumper of the back of the truck, reaching above our heads doing some MacGyver move with the excess slack, that instantly yanks my arms over my head, locking them in place.

My head whips up to look at my hands as I attempt to pull on the restraints which don't budge an inch. He tugs slightly on the middle of the rope, testing his design, then tilts his chin down meeting my gaze with a shit-eating grin.

"These won't leave any marks. Scouts honor." He holds up three fingers, his smile never fading.

Lowering himself with his body flush against mine, his shirt stays in place exposing his perfectly sculpted abs for the second time today and my mouth quite literally waters at the sight.

My eyes graze over the tight lines of his exposed skin and like a total clichè, because I can't help myself, I lick my lips, pulling the bottom one between my teeth while my body sucks in a much needed breath.

The familiar woodsy sage scent engulfs me and my body can't help but respond to not only the compromising position, but the sensual aroma mixed with the watchful eyes of Major and Wade, full of lust and desperation that mirror my own.

Both of them are watching in awe and I can't tear my eyes away from their stalled expressions.

Wade is wide-eyed with his mouth slightly slacked open, as if he needs it to breathe. Major's eyes are squinted, his lustful expression roams over my body and his gaze hovers over my restrained wrists. It's like he's in the midst of his own tortured pain and I don't miss the bulge behind the tight fabric of his pants.

"You say stop, and this all stops. Do you understand?" Jasper says loud enough for everyone to hear.

I look between all the guys and press my lips together because yeah this is me, never saying stop. I nod in understanding anyway and Jasper grins back at me with contagious excitement.

"Good." His smile fades into a smirk as he leans into me. "Now keep your eyes open and on them," Jasper whispers in my ear.

I don't know if I heard him correctly, so I crane my neck back and turn to look at Jasper but his fingers pinch my chin, angling my face back toward Major and Wade.

"Eyes on *them*, Abby." I don't think he's ever called me by my name. Hearing him be assertive and less playful has me obeying his every word like the law-abiding citizen I am.

Except my eyelids almost flutter shut and my jaw slacks open when Jasper kisses the sensitive skin between my ear and collarbone. Slowly tracing his lips over the line of my jaw, stopping inches from my lips before doing the same thing on the other side.

His fingers are gently caressing the sides of my torso that are completely exposed since my arms are stuck straight above my head.

One hand strays, his fingertips gently teasing over the exposed skin between the top of my leggings and hem of my tank top. His hand moves back and forth over my stomach and up the channel in between my breasts, then circles around their shape before moving his fingers back down, sneaking a barely there graze over the peak, making my nipple harden as I suck in a surprised breath.

Naturally, I tilt my chin down to see what he's doing but his other hand cups around the base of my throat preventing me from moving.

"Eyes. On. Them." My eyes snap back over to Major and Wade, both holding expressions similar to my own. Lust dripping from their eyes, jaw slacked and scared to blink.

Jasper rolls his hips into mine, as his erection rubs against me and I can't help but moan.

His body is flush against mine. He begins caressing me with his tongue and fingers under the watchful eyes of two other men and it's both terrifying and exhilarating.

Jasper's hand is still cupped around my neck as his lips graze over mine and he hovers there for a moment. I don't change my line of sight, keeping my gaze locked on the two men watching us but I see Jasper in my periphery, his eyes bouncing between my eyes and lips.

"Don't you dare close your eyes." His whisper is barely audible. "I want you to see how badly they want you." I nod once.

"Tell me you understand?" he asks, since my nod was barely noticeable due to his hand placement.

"Yes," I whisper.

Then he leans in, pressing our lips together with a gentle force that I love. His tongue sweeps over mine, and they dance together in a soft slow rhythm.

I've never been kissed so passionately before or in such a compromising position, especially while being watched like this and it's creating a sensation I can't even begin to describe.

My pulse is racing and it feels like every inch of my body is being doused in gasoline and lit on fire.

As instructed, I keep my eyes open and they're currently locked on Major's intense gaze. The sensation of being kissed by one man while staring into the eyes of another is a sexual high I never knew I needed. His wanton expression is feeding my own desire and I can't help but moan again feeling like I want more from all of them.

Wade's fists clench at his sides and before our Truth or Dare kiss I would have automatically assumed he was pissed off or hated something, but with the way his gaze is trained on me and Jasper, I know he's just trying to prevent from touching himself. The thought sends shockwaves to my core and more uncontrollable, embarrassing sounds come from somewhere in the middle of my chest.

Naturally my hips respond, needing friction and when they roll against Jasper's length, a grunted groan muffles between our lips before he pulls back, pressing his forehead to my chest.

"Fuck, pumpkin." His grip loosens around my neck as he trails it down my body and places both hands around my hips as if to hold me in place. "You feel too good."

He presses his lips against the middle of my chest before stepping back, standing in between Major and Wade.

God, they're a sight.

All three men are a stark contrast physically but they all have that same strong demeanor that commands attention.

Jasper takes another step toward them, waving the guys to come with him, leaving me tied to the back of the fire truck with no ability to move.

"Hey…uh, where are you guys going?"

"Don't go anywhere, pumpkin." Now the playful tone Jasper

typically has is back and that worries me even more in my current predicament.

They turn into the far corner of the garage where the lockers are and disappear from sight.

"Yeah, I'll just…stay right here!" I yell back, using my sarcasm wisely, as my voice echoes through the garage. I glance up, yanking at the restraints and still nothing budges. "Yup, not going anywhere," I whisper under my breath.

The clinging of metal on metal pierces the silence in the garage and some shuffling sounds echo from their direction. My body begins to feel panicked, the anticipation is now verging on anxiety because as much as I've felt comfortable with these guys, I have no idea what to expect.

I've known them for only a few hours and here I am playing Truth or Dare and letting them tie me to the back of a fire truck.

My natural inclination in trusting people is the exact reason why Sam used me the way he did and why I refused to see the glaring signs that were in his hidden agenda.

Yet, here I am letting an almost stranger tie me to a parked vehicle, agreeing to this craziness.

Even with all of my rampant, overthinking thoughts, there's a chemistry between all of us that's impossible to ignore. I feel it. And I really hope I'm not wrong about it.

I glance up at the knots in the rope and realize there's nothing I can do to get out of this. Not that I'm sure I want to but the longer they're gone the more I begin to reprimand myself.

I guess it could be worse. I could be naked.

And all my thoughts fly completely out the window when I see Jasper round the corner of the garage shirtless, wearing only his turnout gear pants with thick red straps being used like suspenders draping over each side of his body, holding them in place.

The tattoos that decorate his lean body are on full display, his chest is fully covered with the ink that snakes underneath the red straps all the way down both his arms stopping at his wrists.

His large, oversized boots and helmet top off his ensemble with only a black and white bandana that hangs from his fingertips.

My jaw drops when Wade and Major turn the corner, trailing right behind with identical uniforms, save the bandana.

It's like I've died and gone to fire station heaven.

Or hell depending on where that bandana is going.

They need their own walk up song or at least some light porno music playing in the background for how delicious they look.

Major's colossal frame has a landscape of muscles and his thick chest curves into his ribcage with perfection. His short hair is hidden underneath his helmet but his amber eyes, full of lust, are blaring bright, searing straight through me.

And Wade, my god, Wade. His shoulders are thick and wide yet proportional to his strong body. I knew he was big, everything about him looks oversized, but seeing the expanse of his olive skin and muscular lines with nothing hiding it, has my body drooling with need.

As if practiced, they all stop in synchronized motion just a few paces in front of me and I'm speechless, contradicting my thoughts that sound like undomesticated, wild animals.

"Memorize what you can, princess. You'll only get one guess and your senses will be limited." Major's deep, commanding voice is like velvet to my ears.

Well, if I'm going to play this game, I'm going all in.

"Turn around so I can see all of you."

They glance at each other, before Major takes the lead and makes a small circle where he stands. Jasper and Wade follow, giving me a 360 degree view of their bodies.

"Take off your helmets," they glance between each other again, "just for a second," I add.

All of them lift their helmets off their heads and I take in exactly how they look. Not only to attempt to win this game but also to sear the sight of these three half naked men into the depths of my soul.

Wade's dark brown hair is styled and compliant with the exception of the floppy section in the front that lays over his forehead. Jasper's dirty blonde, normally messy strands, are tied back in a small man bun, and Major's hair is easily distinct due to how short it is compared to the others.

They place the helmets back on their heads but before Jasper can step forward, I spit out, "drop the suspenders." I know it's not the only thing holding them in place, but they get my gist.

I raise my eyebrows as they all look at me with different expressions. I tilt my head, shaking my wrists at the restraints, reminding them of my compromising position.

Jasper doesn't take his eyes off mine as he unclips something near the front of his pants and pulls off the straps. The thick fabric falls heavily, pooling at his ankles.

My mouth must be made of the same material because it feels just as dry and drops just as quickly seeing Jasper fully naked with nothing covering him, except more tattoos and an impressively hard cock that springs free from its cloth cage.

As my eyes drop down to take in the glorious view of his gorgeous cock, my breath catches in my throat when the dim light bounces off a shiny metal hoop pierced through the tip of his cock.

"This is the only hint you get, pumpkin." He smirks, as he wraps a hand around the base, giving his cock a long, languid pull. His thumb massages the metal bar then his hand retreats back to the base. It's slow and sensual but too fast as he leans down and pulls his pants back up to his waist, securing the straps over his shoulders again and I already feel the loss of the sight.

Stepping forward, he grips the bandana between both his hands as he leans into me.

I sneak a glance over at Wade, the depths of his irises are so much darker than usual and I know Jasper's body had the same effect on him as it did on me.

Shifting my eyeline to Major, I find his gaze still searing into me like he's taking in every second of this and branding it to his memory.

Then everything goes completely dark as Jasper gently lays the strip cloth over my eyes and ties it behind my head.

"It's time to play, pumpkin."

CHAPTER 22
PRINCE ALBERT.
TURNING STRAIGHT
MEN GAY SINCE 1972

WADE

I'm not sure what has gotten into any of us, but as I glance around at the guys, we're all in and couldn't be happier about it.

After Jasper told us his plan about dressing in our turnout gear, it was a full blown competition as to who could get dressed and back out to Abby the quickest.

That's not unusual in our daily life. We're tested to dress in our gear in less than ninety seconds. Jasper, the fucking little ninja, always wins.

But, rounding that corner and seeing Abby strapped to the back of our truck, completely willingly and at our mercy, was a once-in-a-lifetime sight and I'm not going to let my analytical thoughts get the best of me.

I feel more alive than I've felt in years. Then Jasper dropping trow without a second thought was like a double espresso shot straight to my dick.

I've visualized what it would be like to see him naked, to see his cock lay heavy between his legs, with nothing but lust filling his eyes. To see what he looks like in a moment of desperate sexual need.

I've daydreamed about it, more than I'd like to admit but it looks better in real life than I ever expected.

Then, seeing that piercing looped through the top of his cock was like a personal invitation for my mouth. I've never wanted to inspect something with my tongue more than that piercing on his cock.

Jasper is leaning into Abby, whispering something in her ear as his free hand blindly waves behind him, gesturing me over.

It's difficult to be quiet in our turnout gear. The fabric is thick and the friction is like rubbing sandpaper together, but I take a few calculated steps and stand opposite of Jasper without her sensing me.

He tips his chin at me, as his eyes shift to an invisible spot on her face like I'm supposed to know what to do.

I've been with plenty of women in my life, but never with another man pleasing the same woman, much less a third man watching.

My nerves are getting the best of me while I think of all the reasons why we shouldn't be doing this. And why I shouldn't be exploring this curiosity I've had over Jasper. It's reckless and stupid and as my brain begins to retreat so does my body.

I take a small step back but before I can even put my foot back down, Jasper reaches out, grabs the back of my neck and pulls me into him. His lips graze the stubble of my jaw and he makes it known exactly what he is thinking.

"This isn't about you and me, this is about Abby and nothing else. So, get the fuck out of your head." He loosens the hold he has and pulls back, looking me in the eye. "Now, are you going to help me please our girl?"

In our day to day life, it's hard to take Jasper seriously. He's always playful and most often pranking someone or joking around. It's something I've always been drawn to about him.

This is the second time I've seen Jasper in a sexual situation, and it's like watching a cub morph into a lion. I can't say I hate it.

The look in his eye is dark and feral. Not just for Abby but for me as well and I can't say I hate that either. But he's right. My eyes shift over his shoulder to Abby's gorgeous body, tied up in utter perfection up against the back of our truck, waiting to be pleased.

My body instantly relaxes when I see the heavy rise and fall of her chest and hear the almost silent whimper behind her breath. The way her legs squeeze together as she shifts, unable to use any other part of her body to provide relief to her aching core.

She needs us like we need her.

And I never let anyone down.

My lips quirk up in a smile as I peer back at Jasper. It's like we exchange expressions because now the pinch between his brow gives away that he thinks I might be crazy with my shit-eating grin on display.

Cupping my hand, I gently pat the side of his face as I step around him and say, "*Let us turn up the heat*, shall we."

CHAPTER 23
I MIGHT NEED A VOYEURISM SUPPORT GROUP AFTER THIS

MAJOR

Wade whispers something I can't hear to Jasper, then steps in front of Abby as his fingertips roam the exposed area of her stomach.

She's wearing a short, black lace tank top, I think she referred to it as a crop top earlier, that already shows a sliver of her stomach, but with the way her arms are pulled over her head there's a large portion of her torso exposed, showing off her gorgeous olive skin.

For a moment I thought I was going to have to break them apart, as I usually have to do, but when I saw the smile appear across Wade's face I knew he was in the right mindset. And when he's determined, nothing else matters. His strongest personality trait is his drive when he sets his mind to something. Yet, most annoying because he's relentless. And when both he and Jasper team up on me, it's only a matter of time before I have to give in and give them what they want.

It's just not often they're both on the same page, much less getting along like they are now.

Speaking of, I glance down at myself and chuckle internally

wondering how the hell I got into this predicament. I may not be as lean or muscular as Wade or Jasper, but for a man a handful of years into his forties I can't say I'm too far off.

Although Abby doesn't make me feel my age, especially right now.

My favorite part of any sexual act is normally observing, but my body is screaming to join them right now. I'm dying to strip off these ridiculously heavy pants, climb that ladder until my hips line up with Abby's face, and press my cock against her lips, making her taste the pre-cum leaking from the tip.

Thankfully patience is my strong suit and I'm waiting to make my entrance. I quietly step to the side, changing my view as I watch Wade lean closer into Abby. He presses his body into hers as his fingers caress her exposed skin and her mouth is parted open, breath heavy and with her head tilted back, I imagine her eyes are squeezed shut underneath that blindfold, enjoying every unexpected touch.

Wade's fingers dip into the sides of her leggings and he glances over at Jasper. The silent communication that happens naturally between the two of them when we're out in the field is in full working order right now.

"Is this okay?" Jasper asks.

Abby nods and Wade gently pulls her leggings down, inching the fabric slowly off her legs and stripping them off and over her now bare feet. He tosses them aside then trails his hands from her ankles up to her knees as Jasper brushes his hands over her thick thighs and the visible shiver that runs through her body as she lets out a whimper, stirs my already half-hard cock to life.

The gorgeous landscape of tan skin glows as I take in every inch of her stunning body.

The light pink tone of her painted toenails match the color of her lace thong. The loose, black crop top hangs perfectly over the peak of her breasts and I attempt to brand this view to my memory.

"Who's touching you, Abby?" Jasper asks.

"Jasper and Wade," she answers breathy, but confidently.

"You're right, only because you know Major is dying to watch every single thing we do to you, right?" She nods as he runs his fingertip around her navel then over the peak of her breast, teasing around her pert nipple.

"Should we give him a show?" His voice drops deeper as he leans into her like it's a secret between them.

She nods again, and he asks, "Are you sure?" pinching her nipple at the same time.

"Y-yes," she stammers out with more breath than words.

Wade and Jasper exchange looks before they both press their lips to her body, teasing their tongues over opposite sides of her writhing body.

Wade's fingers gently massage around her foot as he places kisses over her ankle and trails up to her thighs.

Jasper starts at her jawline, to her chin, collarbone, then trails over the fabric of her shirt between her breastbone until he's crouched down and his face is flush with her stomach.

Both of them are now level at her waist. Her hands are still extended and tied above her head so taking her top off isn't an option. Instead Jasper gets creative and pulls the front of her top over her head, tucking it behind her neck.

Reaching behind her, he pauses to ask, "Is this okay, pumpkin?"

"Yes," she answers as she nods, making double sure he knows she's on board with this and my cock thickens even more.

I step back and sit down in the chair that faces their direction, because I'm afraid I might pass out from the lack of oxygen as my body stalls for breath with each touch.

It's a lightning speed realization that I don't actually have any patience when it comes to Abby, because I can't help but push down my pants and pull out my aching cock, giving it the attention it's screaming for.

"Fuck, Abby," I unintentionally say out loud, as I pull on the soft skin of my steel shaft.

In synchronized motion, they all turn in my direction. Abby tips her head back in an attempt to sneak a glimpse from behind her blindfold, while Jasper and Wade witness my resolve. I stroke myself, not caring that I'm usually the one watching, not being watched.

Jasper grins, pleased at the fact that we're all completely falling apart, then turns back to Abby. "He's stroking himself for you, pumpkin." Then he unclips the back of her bra strap.

The cups pull up to the top of her chest, as her heavy breasts bounce out of the fabric. Jasper pulls the bra over her head, lining it up with her shirt so it's out of the way and now there's nothing obstructing the view of her round, ample tits and tight nipples.

Jasper and Wade eye each other as they lean into her.

Jasper flicks out his tongue at the peak of her nipple then Wade blows on it, making it pucker and glisten.

Abby jams her mouth shut and moans, like she's trying to stop herself from crying out, but her loud, desperate pant is inevitable when they both wrap their lips around each peak, sucking and licking as they caress her body.

Fuuuuck.

I stop myself from stroking faster, knowing it's been too long and I have to wait this out. Instead pulling long, languid strokes, unable to prevent my stuttering breath and muffled groans.

She writhes under their touch, rolling her hips and tossing her head back and forth. All three moan before Jasper wraps his hand around Wade's forearm, getting his attention and they both pull back at the same time.

Abby's breath hitches with a whimper.

"Why did you stop?" Her neck is blindly swiveling, attempting to find where they went.

They don't answer as they switch spots, silently moving

around each other, and Wade steps forward. He places his fingers between her belly button and the lace fabric of her underwear, then proceeds to slowly dip them inside.

His hand moves down to the apex of her thighs and I can see the outline of his finger under the lace, swiping it between her slit.

She gasps, bucking her hips at the touch and bites at the corner of her lips.

"Oh fuck," she moans. The sound comes from somewhere deep in her soul and I can relate to where it's coming from as I continue to knead my cock.

"Who's touching you, princess?" I ask her, interrupting the silence.

"Jasper," she replies quickly.

"Wrong," Wade says as he pulls his hand free from the fabric, pulling the front of his pants down to swipe a bead of pre-cum on his glistening finger then presses it into her mouth.

"Taste that and remember it. That's me and you, sweetheart. And I'm going to brand the flavor to your tongue so you'll never forget it."

Jasper's wide eyed expression mirrors mine, because he's just as shocked as I am at Wade's possessive response.

Jasper recovers quickly, as his mouth aligns with Abby's. The entire time his gaze is trained on Wade. His tongue darts out over her puckered lips, still stuffed with Wade's fingers and when Wade starts to pull them out, Jasper's mouth engulfs them.

His wet tongue weaves over Abby's lips then Wade's fingers, taking them into his mouth and sucks.

Wade grunts, leans forward and kisses Abby like he has no idea what else to do while Jasper sucks his fingers clean.

"Mmmm, you taste good. Both of you." Jasper drops to his knees, tucking his fingers into the side of Abby's thong, and pulls it completely off.

Pressing her thighs apart he dives in, flattening his tongue over her center, putting pressure over her clit, granting us a moan that echoes through the garage.

Tucking his hand behind her knee, he presses up, spreading one leg even further open. In their perfect, unspoken language, Wade takes over, gripping the back of her knee and pulls her leg up toward her chest, exposing her swollen clit and Jasper feeds off her like a starving man.

Both Wade and I watch as he devours her. Abby's body writhes with need and lust and fuck, I wish I could see her eyes. I want to take that blindfold off so I can watch her eyes roll to the back of her head while her irises blow out right before she climaxes.

Which is soon by the looks of what Jasper is doing to her.

Her breath quickens and moans grow louder. Wade dips his head down, his gaze trained on Jasper's tongue as he darts out his own, lapping at the peak of her nipple.

Abby moans even louder and bucks, attempting to pull at the rope to pull herself away.

"Oh god, I'm close," she cries out, unashamed of her desperation and it's so fucking beautiful.

In that same moment, Jasper pulls away then grips the back of Wade's head and with a handful of hair in his hand, places him down in front of Abby, pressing him into her center.

"Keep her on edge, don't let her come," Jasper threatens in the most Jasper way I've ever heard.

"Don't come yet, pumpkin," he says to Abby, still playful but clearly dead serious.

She knows they swapped but it doesn't appear that she cares when she moans as Wade darts out his tongue, lapping at the mixture of her arousal and Jasper's saliva.

He moans then pulls back and glances up at her bindings. "Grip onto the ladder, sweetheart."

The restraint is snug, but loose enough that she's able to flip her hands around from underneath the rope and wrap her fingers around the metal, holding herself in place. Wade dives back in as he uses his hands to hold the back of her legs, spreading her open.

Jasper steps back, letting the straps of his pants fall over his inked shoulders, then shuffles back toward his locker, kicking them off in the process. His bare ass out like a full moon, as his cock bounces with the stride of his step.

"Oh fuck," Abby moans.

"Don't you dare, Wade!" he shouts through the room as he digs into his bag.

Abby swears under her breath then moans again.

Wade joins her as he exaggerates his own groan, moaning into Abby's pussy loud enough for Jasper to hear.

"Waddddde…" Jasper threatens just as Abby screams.

"Oh, god, I'm coming," Abby wails out and moans through her orgasm as Jasper runs back, grabbing the back of Wade's pants, yanking him back from his kneeling position. He falls on his back as Jasper throws a few condoms on him, giving him a smug yet pissed off wide-eyed expression that only Jasper can master.

"You're both going to pay for that." Jasper places the condom wrapper between his teeth, tearing it open, then sheaths his cock with the rubber casing.

Turning his back to us, he faces Abby and leans into the nook of her neck as he tucks his arms underneath one leg. He lines his cock up against her entrance, tapping the tip over her swollen clit.

"Are you ready for my cock?" he asks, as his hips flex up and down. The back of his pierced shaft rubs against her sensitive pussy causing a friction that makes Abby's breath hitch.

"Y-yes. God, yes." Her answer is choppy but clear as she rolls her hips, silently begging for more.

"Mmmmm, good girl," he praises, pleased with her answer.

Jasper retracts his hips as he lines his cock up with her

entrance and pushes in. Abby's jaw falls open and then slams shut, letting out another long moan. It's echoing in surround sound between my heavy breathing and the moans coming from both Jasper and now Wade.

Jasper pistons his hips, pulling his cock almost all the way out before thrusting back in. His long, sheathed cock shines with her arousal as he dips his chin watching his cock move in and out of her.

"Your tight pussy is clenching my cock, baby. Are you going to come again?"

She nods, pressing her lips in a hard line, like she doesn't want to admit it out loud.

She gasps when he presses his thumb against her clit as he continues thrusting.

Jasper glances over his shoulder as Wade pushes himself off the floor and sits in a folding chair that's about a foot away from mine. Their eyes meet and Jasper tips his chin at his pants then gestures his head to the right.

Wade quietly stands, unbuttons the front and lets the pants fall to the ground. His thick, engorged cock bounces out, as he kicks his turnout gear to the side. Jasper glances down, watching Wade wrap his hand around his hard cock, stroking it from base to tip bringing a bead of pre-cum to the tip.

The feral look in Jasper's eyes matches the wild and carefree attitude he has in his daily life. His jaw slacks open and the way his blown out irises cover his normally bright ocean blue eyes, is like nothing I've ever seen before. He's got a desperate need for both of them and it's the first time Jasper doesn't have the upper hand with Wade.

Wade's smirk knows it, too. Slowly, he sits down on the chair, slouching down as if he's getting comfortable as he continues to give his cock attention.

"Oh, fuck, don't stop," Abby begs and Jasper immediately turns to look at Abby and stops thrusting.

Abby sucks in a breath. "What the hell?" She pulls at her restraints and bucks her hips.

"Next time I tell you not to come, don't come." He reaches over her head and with one hand, unties the knots allowing the rope to unravel from the ladder, freeing her hands.

CHAPTER 24
COCKWARMING IS FOR MASOCHISTS

WADE

My eyebrows hit my hairline when Jasper unties Abby.

Is he going to make us all stop like this?

He was pissed I made Abby come, but he still had that signature playful look he always has when he yanked me off her and tossed enough condoms for a small army at me.

I glance down at myself, wondering where the hell my normally rigid self has gone, but as I peer over to Major in the same position as I am, I feel justified in my abnormal reaction.

Every single one of us is all in for this and, at this point, nothing is going to stop us.

Except Jasper, whose actions are expected based on his typical unpredictable behavior.

He silently nods at my hand holding the condom, then tips his chin at my achingly, hard cock, and I know he's not done with whatever it is we're doing.

I take in a deep breath, both to calm myself and provide the normalcy of being overly irritated like I usually am with him, but still listen to his unspoken command as I tear open the wrapping and pull the latex ring over my crown. Keeping my eyes on

Jasper, I give myself a leisurely stroke from the tip to the base as I roll it on.

There's a glint of lust in Jasper's expression and fuck, I love the desire burning behind them. He grants me a crooked smile clearly pleased with my compliance, then he turns his attention back to Abby untying the ropes, allowing her arms to move freely. She pulls her hands into her chest, wrapping one hand around her wrist, still blindfolded.

"Still trust me?" Jasper asks her as he takes a moment to remove her shirt and top that was wrapped around her arms and neck like a figure eight.

She nods, as he brings his hands to her waist, hoisting her flush against him. Her legs naturally wrap around him as her arms drape over his shoulders and circle around the back of his neck.

He takes a step back as he turns around, walks toward me, then stops in between my spread legs.

I trail my eyes down the gorgeous lines of her back and over the round curves of her even more beautiful ass as he slowly squats down and leans slightly forward, lining her up with my erect cock. As my tip presses into her pussy, she gasps with both surprise and pleasure.

I grip onto her hips, allowing Jasper to let go and she eases down on the length of my shaft painfully slowly. I grunt, throwing my head back as she moans and Jasper fucking smiles, like he knows some secret we don't. Which I know he does because he probably has some crazy idea that I'm going to fucking hate but love at the same time.

Bringing his hands behind Abby's head, he unties the bandana that's been covering her eyes. I crane my neck to see the entirety of her gorgeous face, and fuck, she's stunning. Even with the screwed up expression on her face, as she squints and blinks heavily, she's breathtaking. As she looks over her shoulder, her eyes widen and brows raise. I think she's surprised to see it's me and not Major, but clearly pleased as she gives a slight roll of her hips over my cock. My jaw drops as I push into her, making not only the two of us moan but Major as well.

She turns to look in his direction, then places her hands on my thighs for leverage, rolling her hips once again and I can't help but grip her hips harder. "Fuuuuuuck," leaves my lips with a lengthy moan.

"She feels so good, doesn't she?" Jasper says as he takes a step back, tossing the bandana on the floor.

Abby rounds her hips deeper over my cock and Jasper's more than right. She feels unbelievable.

"Stop moving," Jasper instructs, his voice deep and serious.

We both halt our movement and whiplash our necks in his direction.

"Do. Not. Move," he says each word with exact pronunciation, then reaches out pressing one finger against her chin, turning her gaze to Major.

She glances down at his engorged cock, his fingers wrapped around the shaft as he strokes himself base to tip.

We change our clothes in front of each other all the time, but most often we all have boxers or briefs on. It's shocking to see Major completely naked and unhinged as he watches us. What's more shocking, the size of his goddamn goliath cock.

I would say we're all decently sized. Mine is above average with a bit more girth than average, Jasper is longer but leaner than mine.

But Major. Major's dick is like the fucking empire state building. Rock hard, impossible to miss, standing tall between his thick thighs and spread legs.

His gaze stays locked on Abby, and solely her, which is standard behavior for Major. He hyper focuses on whatever he's doing or working on, both personally and professionally, and clearly Abby has his undivided attention right now.

He seems comfortable and at ease, just like Jasper is. Both fully in control.

So, it appears I'm the only one completely out of element and acting totally out of character.

"Wade," Jasper says my name, his voice huskier than usual, and it pulls me back into the moment.

Turning my attention to him, he keeps one hand on Abby's chin held in Major's direction, while the other strokes himself and I can't help but dip my gaze down, watching the delicate yet punishing way he pleases himself. I swallow thickly as my cock twitches and Abby shifts in response as she whimpers.

"I said don't move, Abby, and keep your eyes on him."

She bites her lip and whines. One that's both from need and frustration. Her chest lifts as she sucks in a commanding breath, blowing it out slowly through her slightly parted lips. She's dying for more and so am I. This is fucking unbearable.

My gaze drifts back to Jasper while Abby's are glued to Major's. My hard cock is still painfully hard and parked in her throbbing pussy and we can't do anything about it.

I run my hand through my hair, gripping painfully at the roots. Fuck, I want to move. I *need* to move.

Jasper's *payback* is pure torture.

"Clench around his cock," Major instructs Abby and his words are as commanding as his gaze, because she easily obeys as her walls seize my dick and it throbs instantly.

"Umpf, fuck," I grit out. I feel tormented in ways I've never experienced. The desire to pound into her is indescribable and I consider begging Jasper to let me move, giving him anything he wants if I was granted permission to do so.

I steady my breath as my eyes peer over to Jasper. I follow the movement of his hand, mesmerized by the way his abs contract when his fingers twist over the crown. The coiled piercing flips back and forth, while pre-cum leaks out of the tip and over the polished metal.

He leans his head back with an intentional groan, teasing us further and the powerplay pisses me off. Not in the normal way he pisses me off, but as I glance at Abby feeling as tortured as I do, I know I need to get some payback myself.

With a mind of its own, my hand inches toward Jasper. He catches the movement then shifts his gaze to me and our eyes lock at the exact moment my fingers wrap around his cock.

CHAPTER 25
MANIPULATION AT ITS FINEST

JASPER

"Oh f-fffuuuucckk." My eyes roll to the back of my skull and I swear they explode behind my head.

Wade is touching me. A very straight Wade is touching *me*.

I don't know what this means but I'm reveling in every goddamn second of it.

My jaw drops open as my hips pump into his large, calloused hand. Fuck, he feels good.

Apparently I said that out loud because Abby dips her chin out of my grasp and turns her attention to me.

She's got an eye level view of his hand on my cock, leisurely stroking it like he doesn't have a care in the world and by the look on said straight man's face, he's enjoying every minute of this power exchange.

I quickly turn my attention back to Abby to study her expression. Having a man touch me isn't new to me. But I know it's new to Wade and I assume Abby, too.

I've been holding back with him in fear he would freak out. But here he is diving head first, turning my brain to mush and melting all of my willpower. I definitely wasn't planning for this and although Major may have expected it, I have no idea how she'll respond.

Sure, she dared us to kiss earlier. But that's totally different from what's happening right now.

My jaw drops as his wrist twists around the tip, then strokes back down the length pulling the foreskin tight and flush against my shaft.

I can't help the shattered grunt that falls from my lips but I hear it in stereo when Wade lets out his own tortured grunt.

"Jesus. Fuck, she's clenching around me," he says while squeezing his eyes shut.

His hold tightens as he tugs harder. I pump into his hand, and stumble forward, landing one step closer to both of them.

"You like that, pumpkin?"

She nods, her gaze bouncing between mine and the hand wrapped around my cock.

"Can I move now, please?" she asks as she leans forward, sticking out her tongue, flattening it under my shaft then her lips circle over the tip, sucking it like a goddamn lollipop.

"Mmmmmm. Fuck." An animalistic, garbled noise and infinite profanities bubble out of me. I swear to fucking god they must have spoken telepathically between each other, knowing exactly how to break me. Because I'm fucking eviscerated from head to toe.

I nod rapidly, not caring about anything but his hand and her mouth.

She rolls her hips over Wade's lap and moans. The vibration hits the thinned skin of my achingly hard cock and rolls through my entire body like an endless ripple. I clench my teeth, biting back another groan, as every muscle in my body contracts because this is the hottest thing I've ever experienced.

Considering I've been referred to as a manwhore a few times in my life, it says a lot.

But it has nothing to do with the action and everything to do with the combination of the four of us giving into each other.

Abby moans again when Wade grabs a hold of her hips and thrusts into her. It forces her to lean forward and my cock slides further down her throat.

"Fucking hell." Running my fingers through her silky strands I grip the side of her head, attempting to control her movement to a bearable pace, so I don't come too quickly.

But that's fucking useless. I've been on the edge since I jerked Wade off in his room earlier today, got closer to the cliff when Abby double dared us and now this.

I'm surprised I haven't spontaneously combusted into a million pieces.

I pull away from both of them, heaving as I lean forward, gripping one hand around my cock while the other presses into the top of my thigh for support.

"Feeling okay there, Jas?" Wade asks with a shit eating grin on his face.

This fucker.

His now free hand moves in between Abby's spread legs and his middle finger grazes over her clit.

"Oh, fuck…yes," she wails out as her fingers pinch her nipples and jesus fucking christ the view is unbelievable.

I side-eye a glance at Major. His normally tight posture is slouched in his chair, legs spread wider than the Grand Canyon, mouth agape. His eyes are hooded and his cock is leaking pre-cum like it's a goddamn water fountain.

Wade seems to be the only one in any type of control and I just can't have that.

I drop to my knees in between Wade's spread legs and Abby's glistening center. I knock Wade's hand away and dive in without warning.

She gasps when I lock my lips onto that magical bundle of nerves, flicking my tongue over her center. I suck and lick as I place my hands on the insides of his thighs spreading them both wider which makes her open up for me even more.

She moans as she bucks into my mouth and I have a direct line of sight of Wade's cock sliding in and out of her.

I pull back, circling my thumb over her clit, then flatten my tongue licking down over Wade's balls and suck them into my mouth.

"Ahhhh, Fuuuucccckkk." He flinches and groans, then freezes with his head tossed back and mouth clenched shut. He has a white knuckle grasp on Abby's hips as if attempting to hold her in place but she continues to roll her hips as I keep sucking and licking his balls while circling my finger over her clit.

"Jasper. Stop. Fuck, you're gonna make me come." His admission only feeds my desire to keep going. Abby presses her lips together as she squeezes her eyes shut and I know she's on the verge as well. I reach down with my free hand moving my mouth and fingers at a punishing pace, matching the strokes on my own cock as they both fall off the cliff.

"I can't hold back anymore. Fuck!" Wade roars as his orgasm hits him.

Abby whispers underneath her heavy breath while looking down at me. Her mouth wide open as her brows pinch together. "Fuck, I'm coming."

"Eyes on me when you come, princess," Major says with a calm I'm jealous of.

Her head jerks in his direction and I pull back, pressing my forehead against the side of Wade's thigh. My hand pumps my cock needing a release like I need my next breath.

I peer up at Wade, and his blown out, satiated pupils meet mine. My orgasm hits me like an unstoppable freight train and I grunt into his leg, as hot white ropes spurt and spill over my wretched cock.

"Fuck," I breathe out.

A few seconds pass, a minute maybe. The air is dense and

my ears are dull. The sounds around me are muffled and I can hardly hear anything. Even my vision is blurred from how tight my eyelids were squeezing shut.

I blink and open my jaw as if to pop my ear drums. "Wow," is literally all I can come up with. It's stupid but my brain is no longer a fully functioning organ.

Silence fills the space around me, hearing only our labored breath and my pounding pulse.

I peer up, appraising the lines of Abby's gorgeous face. Her tan skin is slightly flushed and glowing. A light sheen of sweat glistens over her high cheekbones as she bites the corner of her lip. Her eyes are locked in Major's direction and as I follow her line of sight I see the distinct motion of his long languid strokes.

His deep, commanding voice breaks the silence. "Come here, princess, it's my turn."

CHAPTER 26
CONFIDENCE IS THE SEXIEST OUTFIT

ABBY

I have no idea what has gotten into me. But I don't seem to care when I push myself off Wade's lap and take a step in Major's direction.

I saunter toward him, riding on a wave of bliss after what just happened. The undivided attention from two of the sexiest men I've ever laid my eyes on.

Having them both touch me as I tried to figure out who was who, might be a new sexual addiction and I have no idea how that will be outdone.

But also, knowing Major was completely wretched, groaning and touching himself while watching each and every move. I hum a pleased moan to myself at the thought, as I crouch down to pick up a condom on my way over to him.

Speaking of sexy men.

I take a final step, stopping directly in front of his still spread legs. He hasn't stopped stroking himself since our eyes locked and he called me over. Not once has his gaze strayed in any other direction.

His behavior now is the same as it's been since the moment we met. Wholly, undivided and completely attentive.

I trail my eyes down his face and over his body. His lips are parted and his breath is heavy. The golden hue of his skin glows with the light sheen of sweat covering it. One hand is gripping tightly around his hip while the other continues to slowly stroke himself.

My eyes widen as I study him and not because his stroke is painfully slow but because his cock is huge. It's both long and thick and by far the biggest one I've seen in real life.

I thought Jasper's was big and I could feel how large Wade was but Major is on a whole other level.

I glance back over my shoulder to get another look at the two of them. Surprisingly both are hard again, touching themselves as they stare in our direction.

Jasper's is long with that sexy curve and even sexier piercing straight through the tip of his shaft. A shiver runs through me recalling how it felt rubbing against the inside of my walls as he made me come.

Wade's isn't as long as Jaspers, but wider and both are absolutely perfect.

But Major, I turn back to look at the monster sized cock, is fucking intimidating.

"Do you like what you see?"

I nod, because I do, but I have no idea how that thing is going to fit inside me.

Tearing open the condom wrapper, I suck the latex tip into my mouth and crouch down between his legs as I press the circular ring over the top and press my head forward, rolling the condom over the tip.

He bares his teeth as he hisses, "Fuuuuuck."

This normally, well-put together man is easily falling apart for me, and I have to admit, the control is sort of addicting. I smile up at him, using my hand to roll the rest of the latex over his hard length and his jaw falls open.

Yup. Completely addicting and it's giving me a confidence I usually don't have when it comes to situations like these.

Who am I kidding? I have never been in this kind of situation.

Still our eyes stay locked and I can't help my amused smile as I stare back at him.

"You like having this kind of power over me, princess?"

I nod as I bite my lip. "I do. It's like you're my own personal prince charming, always watching out for me." I give him a fitting nickname, considering the one he's given me, but by the wildfire that ignites behind his eyes I can tell that was a mistake.

Leaning forward, his finger crooks under my chin lifting it so we're eye to eye. His eyes laser through me as his dark irises flood the rich amber of his pupils.

"I might call you princess but I'm no prince charming. I'm your king. Now, come sit on my cock." He leans back, inviting me in, and my body wants nothing more than to obey.

I step over each side of his legs and straddle his hips. Draping my arms over his shoulders, he guides me down over his cock and I screw up my face with a muffled groan.

"Fuck, it's too big," I grit out.

"Breathe for me, baby," he says as he guides me further down on him.

"Mmmm," I hear moaning from Wade or Jasper, I don't know which. I'm too focused on not completely losing my lungs.

My body clenches around him trying to stop the intrusion.

He groans and pauses as he grips my hips.

We both stop, fighting both the pleasure and the pain. Our labored breath swims between us as his eyes lock on mine.

"Still with me, princess?"

God, how do four little words sound so goddamn sexy?

I take another deep breath in, letting the air out slowly through my mouth and nod as I seat myself fully in his lap.

I'm flush against him now and frozen in place. I feel so full, I swear all my organs have been rearranged inside my body.

"Hold onto me." He presses into his heels and stands up, lifting me like a helium balloon. Passing by both Wade and Jasper, he leans me up against the side of the fire truck, pulls out to the tip, then pistons into me.

"Oh, fuck." I toss my head back as his cock thrusts in and out of me. It's still monstrous but it feels better than the first time. My walls contract around him as I squeeze my eyes shut and moan again.

"You feel so good around my cock, so perfect," he praises, even though I don't need the words, they feed my soul. I feel so wanted by all of them, needed even. Like it's important to them that I'm here.

"Major, please," I beg, not even sure what I'm asking for.

"I know, princess." He pulls out, thrusting back in, this time continuing the pace and my body welcomes it.

Wade stands, tilting his head in our direction attempting to get a better view of us, still stroking a now fully hard cock. Jasper is still leaning back on one hand as he strokes himself, gazing up at Wade.

I want them to continue what they started earlier and I want to see them fall apart for each other as I fall apart for Major. I have no idea what's happening with all of us but I do know that Wade and Jasper have unfinished business.

Major glances back over his shoulder as he notices where my attention is snagged, then says loud enough for all of us to hear, "Tell them what you want."

They look at each other as I appraise them, then Jasper's eyes lock with mine.

I say the first thing that comes to mind. The first thing I thought of after their kiss.

"Suck his cock."

CHAPTER 27

NEW KINK UNLOCKED

JASPER

I lose my breath when I hear Abby's words.

Suck his cock.

I've always been open in the bedroom playing both a submissive or dominant role depending on the mood or partner. But Abby saying those words as she looks me dead in the eye is a new kink I never knew I needed.

My cock twitches at the thought and I shift my position as I sit up on my knees, unintentionally bringing myself closer to Wade and said cock.

Sensing my movement he whips his head in my direction, taking a step back with a worried expression and half scowl on his face.

That's something I'm used to with him, but I'm entirely more vulnerable than usual in this state and I can't help but feel disappointed. My heart skips a beat, fearful of pushing him away or him saying something that will end up breaking me.

Even though I think he wants it, I won't push it. The look of dread and fear blanket his face and as I glance over at Major and

Abby fucking in pure bliss against our truck, I want nothing more than to keep it that way.

So I sit back on my heels and continue to stroke myself like his rejection isn't killing me inside. I'm fighting against my usual take-charge instincts because maybe Abby is our middle ground and the only way I'll ever get to have Wade is if she's with us. I would be fine with that but all the *what if's* flash through my mind and now I'm terrified that what we've done today has ruined everything between us and he'll want nothing to do with me after she leaves.

CHAPTER 28

JUST TAKE THE FUCKING STEP

WADE

I stare at Jasper, wanting so badly to walk over to him, place myself in front of him like an unmovable statue, and let him do exactly what Abby wants.

But I have no idea what it means for us if I do. And more importantly, what happens after this. I know exactly what my body wants as it thrums with need, something that I haven't felt in…well, ever. I don't think I've ever felt this turned on, this desperate for someone, or someones, in this case.

I want Jasper just as much as I want Abby, and having Major in the mix is a security blanket I think we all need. I just hate admitting all of that.

So, I stay back, watching the man I've been lusting over stroke himself, begging my rooted feet to take a step toward him.

My pulse beats heavily in my neck as my breath quickens. It rises with the sound of Abby's moaning as Major whispers in her ear. I can't hear everything he's saying but based on her groans and whimpers, he's dirty talking her into the next universe, telling her exactly what she does to him.

God, she's fucking stunning. The muscles in her thick legs

flex with each thrust as she grips tighter around his waist. Major's back muscles flex each time he pulls back using more of his upper body to hold her against the truck and the two of them together is otherworldly.

Somehow her petite frame fits perfectly within his large one and it makes me wonder how Jasper and I would look together. The thought stirs my cock back to life and my foot slides a millimeter in Jasper's direction.

I can do this.

I want him.

I want him so fucking bad.

My foot pivots, but just as I talk myself into taking a step toward him, Major growls into Abby's neck as he comes. Abby's arms wrap around his back, her fingers clench around his skin and her nails dig into the sensitive flesh as she screams through her own orgasm.

Fuck.

I never thought I'd enjoy watching a woman I'm with get railed by my co-workers but here I am, cock-at-the-ready, hoping this isn't the last time because I'm secretly begging for more.

"Come on, princess. Let's go get you cleaned up." Major steps back from the truck as he carries Abby down the hallway toward the bathroom.

I glance over at Jasper, silently begging him with my eyes to disregard any choice I have and take my cock in his mouth, sucking until I come down his throat. Do what he normally does and be persistent—push all my buttons—because this time, I want him to force me to give in to him.

But Jasper doesn't look in my direction, his eyes don't even blink my way as he gets up. He remains silent as he grabs a stray towel covering himself up, then walks down the hallway and disappears from sight.

CHAPTER 29
AREN'T WE ALL VOYEURS IN SOME WAY

MAJOR

"How are you feeling?" I ask cooly, even though it feels like a Looney Toon character wants to skydive out of my body.

I watch the suds dribble down her skin as the steam bellows around us. I was going to wait to ask that after I was done washing her off but my usual patience is non-existent after everything that just happened.

"Good," she says with a light chuckle, "surprisingly really good. I've never done anything like that before, so I think I'm still taking it all in."

"Neither have I," I reply, as I lather more soap in my hands and rub them over her shoulders.

She spins around, granting me a questioning look that forces me to pause and I gaze into her gorgeous brown eyes. She pulled her curtain of hair into a messy bun that sits on top of her head, except for the few rebel strands that outline her cheeks.

"You guys have never done that before?" Her brows knit as she asks.

"No, we've never done anything like that, ever." My

response is quick and natural because it's the truth and I would hate for her to feel like this is something we just do on a leisurely Friday night.

"That surprises me," she replies honestly.

I can understand her confusion. We're three single firemen that hang out all the time. I can only imagine the assumptions that have gone through her head. But the truth is, everything that happened tonight has nothing to do with us and everything to do with her.

There's something about *her*. Something we all needed that brought us together like that.

I know the old fashioned dating faux pas. Wait three days to call, don't share too much early on, appear interested but not *that* interested.

But I have no interest in playing any games or letting standardized *"rules"* pave the way here.

"I speak for all of us when I say we're going to court the hell out of you."

That makes her giggle and I swear everything she does is either top notch sexy or stupidly adorable.

"Well, old man, the fact that you just used the word 'court'..." Her eyebrows raise playfully.

"Oh, get out of this shower brat, you're clean." I give her ass a light smack and she squeals as she steps out of the enclosure.

It's small, and frankly I'm surprised we both fit in here as comfortably as we did. It just goes to show that she fits everywhere with us.

She grabs a towel, wrapping it around her body and pulls the clip out of her hair. Her silky strands fall easily over her shoulders as she shakes her head back and forth. It's like a live action shampoo commercial, and I'm all here for it.

I don't realize I'm staring until she asks, "So, do you always like to watch?"

I turn my unintentional gaze away and finish tucking the towel around my waist.

Am I ashamed? No. But, my ex-wife's words repeat in my head. The ones accusing me of being a creep who couldn't love a woman if he likes to watch her get fucked by other men.

Yet, here I am falling head first for a woman that I just witnessed experiencing the ultimate pleasure from my two best guys and I can't keep my heart from stuttering out of my chest.

I run my hand through my hair and rub the back of my neck.

"I…" My words stall as I try to find my breath and the right thing to say because I feel nervous about admitting this out loud to another woman.

"I liked watching you watch us," she interrupts, ripping any remaining air from my lungs. "I liked it a lot, actually." A blush forms over her cheeks as she looks down gnawing at the inside of her mouth.

"Really?" I fictionally punch myself in the face for my tone. It sounded questionable, almost judgmental. "I mean, you did?" I ask, softly.

She nods, still glancing down at the floor. "I'm not sure what history there is between Jasper and Wade but I liked watching that, too," she admits.

Me too, actually. More than I expected.

"This thing between them is new. You've brought out something that's been stewing under the surface for quite a while, and it's about fucking time, too. Maybe they'll be able to be in the same room together without killing each other."

She tosses her head side to side slowly, questioning my statement. "Ooooor, one of them is currently in a headlock in the other room."

"Yeah." I chuckle. "We should probably go check on them."

I step toward her, grab her in my arms and press my lips to hers. I can't seem to help myself around her and I both hate, and love, the loss of control.

Kissing her is exactly like it felt the first time. Like a sin-filled addiction and I have no idea if I can ever live without it.

She hums as she pulls away. Her eyes are still closed as her lips ghost over mine, hovering over each other like they never want to break apart.

"Good idea," I say, but take it right back.

"Actually, that's a horrible idea," I scoop her up in my arms, our towels slipping away. Mine falls away completely, while hers hangs on only by a corner caught in our grasps. She squeals and laughs as I take her into my room and envision all the ways I could make her fall apart.

Just as I place her on the bed, a door slams, echoing through the hallway and we both pause, glancing at each other.

"Okay, you're right, let's go check on them," I say as I push myself up and hold my hand out to her.

Time to put out another fire.

CHAPTER 30
FEARLESS WADE IS A FORCE OF NATURE

JASPER

"What the fuck is your problem?" His words sink in and I rear back, shocked from not only his question but the way he barreled into our room, slamming the door behind him.

What the fuck is my *problem?*

I said nothing after he wordlessly rejected me with his disgusted body language and nauseated facial expression. For the first time in my life, I didn't retort back with him, yet every time I do it pisses him off.

I simply walked away this time. I walked away because I'm trying to respect his boundaries and now he's pissed I stayed quiet.

"I can't fucking win with you, Wade." I toss the towel aside, snatch up a pair of joggers and step into them haphazardly yanking them on.

"What the hell does that mean?" he asks, but I think he knows exactly what that means. In fact, I have no idea why he's even fighting me on this.

Sure, I think he's curious. Actually, I know he is. But, he's going to push back on every single thing that happens between us with or without Abby and frankly, my self-esteem can't handle it.

I'm not going to tell him that, though.

I mindlessly pick through my closet for a shirt as I peer in his direction. He's still dressed in his turnout gear, well, half dressed. His lower half is covered by the pants that hang low on his waist, the suspenders are draped over the sides as one hand grips the strap.

His chest, his stupid gorgeous chest, glistens with a light sheen of sweat peppered with the perfect amount of hair between his pecs and, fucking hell, my body can't help but have a visceral reaction to him. Something I've always been good at hiding, but failed at miserably today.

My usual banter with Wade usually fuels me. It's fun to see his reaction and get under his skin. We can debate and rally back and forth about anything and everything, then turn around and be the best working mates in the field. We contrast each other perfectly.

But right now, after everything that's happened today, I have no energy for it.

"It doesn't mean anything," I reply, defeated because I don't have the ability to hide my emotions. Even when I intentionally show them, it comes out as flirtatious and fun, so I'm hardly ever taken seriously.

"Wow, the almighty witty Jasper doesn't have anything more to say," he replies, poking at me.

I rip the shirt off the hanger and throw it across the room then stomp over toward him.

"What the fuck do you want me to say, Wade?" I stand toe to toe with him as he backs further into the wall next to the door. He's hardly made it a foot in the room, like he's unsure he even wants to be here.

We're both still fucking topless, half-horny, half-pissed, and overflowing with testosterone. This is a really bad mixture.

"Want me to tell you how fucking bad I wanted to get down on my knees in front of you? How I fucking daydream about that, non-fucking-stop, but force myself not to, so you don't have an existential crisis? Want me to tell you how bad I want Abby, you, and all of this?" I suck in a desperate breath just to huff it back out again.

"Fuck." I run my hand through my hair, pissed that I admitted everything I was trying to hide, then reach for the door-knob and open the door. "Well, there you go. Did you get what you came for?"

"Not even close," he says under his breath, then dips his fingers into my waistband pulling me flush against him, slamming his lips against mine. My eyes saucer in surprise before squeezing shut and I moan into his mouth.

Jesus fucking christ. My body is on fire and everything tingles. Letting go of the door knob I grab his waist and rock my hips into him, pressing my erection against his.

Fuck.

I pull away, catching my breath as I stare into his dark eyes, burning with so much heat I can feel it against my skin.

"Show me." His words take a minute to register. My brows knit, then soften in realization of what he's asking for. He presses his palm over my shoulder, gently guiding me down in front of him.

"Show me everything you daydream about."

CHAPTER 31
THEY SAY FOUR IS THE PERFECT NUMBER

ABBY

Major suddenly stops, and I collide into his back with the grace of a baby giraffe.

"Why did you—" He holds out his arm, turning as he presses a finger to his lips, shushing me, then points to the door.

It's propped open a couple of feet and we have a direct side view of Wade. He's leaning up against the side of the wall, face-to-face with Jasper. Wade's arm is extended out, at first glance you might think he's pushing Jasper away but it's slightly bent and there's a lightness to his touch.

Their eyes are focused solely on each other and I can feel the undeniable sexual energy that radiates between them, as Jasper cautiously sinks down in front of him.

Wade's chest is heaving in slow motion and it looks like it's taking every ounce of his energy to stay under control.

Major takes a step around me, leaning up against the hallway wall then pulls me into him.

He's almost a foot taller than me and rests his chin on the crown of my head as he wraps his arms around my waist.

Leaning down, his lips graze the shell of my ear as he whispers, "You said you liked watching too, right?" I nod unable to take my eyes off of them, as one of Major's hands covers my mouth and the other dips into my leggings.

A whimper escapes the barrier of his palm and he presses harder into his grip.

"Are you sure?" Jasper asks just loud enough for us to hear as he peers up at Wade.

His jaw is slacked and eyes wide as he curtly nods back.

Jasper folds his fingers into the elastic band of his fire pants and easily pulls them down. His hard cock springs free, bouncing just inches away from Jasper's face.

An audible swallow passes between them as they wait for each other to make a move. Jasper's hands roam up the tops of Wade's legs, as he licks his lips still waiting for more permission.

My eyes volley between them, both on edge just waiting for the other as Major swipes his finger over my wet slit. Arousal pools between my legs and I whimper again, just waiting for what feels like forever for one of them to do something.

They need this. They need this for each other and I silently beg for them to give in.

Just take the leap.

"I want it, Jasper. I want you." A boyish grin passes over Jasper's face as Wade threads his fingers through Jasper's messy hair and inches him forward slowly.

"I'm going to make it so good for you," Jasper says as his mouth opens with a needy groan and he takes Wade's cock all the way down his throat.

"Oh, fuuuuck," Wade stutters through an intense groan, throwing his head against the wall with a thud and hisses.

I roll my hips, needing more friction, needing more anything. I'm just as high watching them now as I was when I was blind-folded by them.

Everything that has happened today was so unexpected and my heart soars with both happiness and worry. Because in one day, these three beautiful men have shown me so much pleasure, admiration, and respect. I feel closer to them than I do anyone else in my life and that thought is both hopeful and depressing.

How can the connection I feel with them rival that of some of my longest friends?

They've treated me like I'm theirs, like I'm part of their family. Like they want me here.

I have no idea how I'll ever experience anything like this again and I never want it to stop.

Major moans in my ear, his hard shaft pressing into my ass as I round my hips over his. Wade thrusts his hips forward with a white knuckle grip on Jasper's hair and pistons into him in perfect rhythm with us.

It's like we're all in sync with each other and I can feel the synergy everywhere.

"You feel so good." Wade squeezes his eyes shut. "Goddammit, Jasper. I won't last long," he hisses again. His eyes snap open and he lifts his head off the wall, glaring down at Jasper with Wade's usual scowl. "Jesus, okay, stop. I'm going to come. Fuck." Wade's grip tightens and he attempts to push him away but Jasper takes a hold of his hips pulling him closer.

Jasper's nose is flush against Wade's skin as he peers up at him. He bobs his head back and forth, his eyes never leaving Wade's face, like he's committing the image to memory.

Wade's eyes flutter as they roll to the back of his head. His jaw drops open, then he drops his head looking down at Jasper, as he takes every inch of his hard cock.

"Fuck. I'm coming." Wade's hips jut forward, his teeth clench and he grunts through his orgasm. Jasper muffles through a moan that mirrors my own.

Major cups his hand tighter over my mouth while he nuzzles his face into my neck, presses kisses along the sensitive skin. His hips push into me again as his fingers circle over my clit and I explode, falling over the edge with Wade. Major moans with my muffled cry, providing a surround sound of grunts and groans. It's like a perfect soundtrack of need and desire and I don't know if I've heard anything sexier in my entire life.

My vision blurs through my orgasm and stars burst behind my eyes. Every orgasm has gotten better than the last and it's terrifying if this is the trend, because I might die of restless vagina syndrome, if this continues. After meeting these guys, I'm certain that's a real disease.

As my vision clears, Major removes his hand from my mouth as he pulls my frazzled hair behind my ear.

"You're so beautiful when you come." He trails his lips over my jaw and I melt into him.

We all are. Is what I want to say, because I've never been so addicted to seeing someone, or someones, come until now. All of them have every ounce of my attention and I smile taking in the view of the four of us satiated and happy.

Jasper kneels back, sitting on his heels still gazing up at Wade. Wade chipmunks his cheeks and blows out a steady breath as his mouth quirks up into a giddy grin.

Wade. Is. Smiling.

"I—" Wade starts to speak but pauses hearing the sound of a creaking door coming from some distance away. I heard it too, but have no idea where it came from.

Wade's brows pinch together as he turns to look through the open door, and sees me and Major still standing against the wall of the hallway. Our eyes connect as we hear someone call out.

"Wade, are you here?" a woman's voice echoes through the narrow space from the garage.

All of us gasp a sharp expression as Wade's eyes blanket with panic.

I glance down at myself and Major, we're both fully dressed as we push ourselves off the wall and straighten up. I look back at Wade, shirtless and his pants are around his ankles, while Jasper sits naked, completely frozen in front of him.

"Daddy?" a smaller voice follows the woman's voice and Wade's face falls.

His foot presses into Jasper's chest, kicking him further away, then he pushes himself off the wall, grabbing the side of the door and slamming it shut.

CHAPTER 32

MOUNTAINS AREN'T FUNNY, THEY ARE HILL AREAS

WADE

Fuck. Fuck, fuck.

My body jerks forward, simultaneously lifting my foot pushing the base into Jasper's chest propelling him away from me. Grabbing the door jamb I slam it shut, just as I see Major passing the hallway calling out for my sister.

She can't see me like this.

She can't see me like this.

How could I be so stupid? So careless? Rachel told me she was going to bring Lily by to say goodnight since it's Christmas Eve.

"Fuck," I belt out as I kick off my pants and rush over to the closet grabbing the first thing I can find.

"Jesus, Wade," Jasper says incredulously, pressing his palm over the area where I kicked him.

I almost miss the roll of his eyes and shake of his head as I pull the shirt over my head and Gumby my arms through it.

"Did you just roll your eyes at me like a petulant child? Like it's not a big deal she could have seen us?

"She *didn't* see us. You're overreacting." He presses his palms into the floor, pulling his legs forward as he pushes himself up. He stands to his full height, grabbing his turnout pants with him.

His tone and body language is far too Jasper'y and calm. He's so nonchalant about everything.

"Nothing is a big deal to you, is it? Do you care about anything at all?" His neck snaps up to meet my gaze. His eyes sink into me, forcing me to swallow thickly.

There's a depth to his eyes I've never seen before. A disappointed dip in his brow that hits me square in the chest. I know how passionate he is. How loyal he is and how much he loves the people around him. But I can't see straight or feel anything but shame right now for being so fucking irresponsible.

"I care about everything!" he yells back, his voice pained. "All I've ever done is push down my feelings and walk on eggshells around you because I care more about you than I do about myself."

Jasper's typical playfulness is gone, replaced by a rage that's so unlike him.

He would always go out of his way to give me more shit than others, using his natural flirtation to poke at me. I thought it was because he liked to rile me up. Get a response out of me. But gazing into his eyes it's so much more than that, it's always been. I think I've always known it, but I can't focus on that right now. I need to go get Lily.

"It doesn't matter, Jasper. Abby's leaving soon and whatever this is," I shake my head, placing my hands on my hips, hating the confession, "it doesn't matter, because it's not going to happen again."

"Don't fucking do that. Don't act like you didn't want this," his hand gestures between the two of us, "and don't assume you know what Abby wants, she—"

"I can't do this, Jasper." I run my hands through my hair. "I can't fucking do this." I push my sockless feet into my shoes, hating the sensation. Hating everything I'm feeling.

"Can't do what? Something for yourself for once?" he continues to poke, but not in the playful Jasper way I'm used to and I don't know how to handle it. He steps toward me, blocking the doorway and I steel my spine, immediately feeling defensive.

"Get out of my way."

"No."

I tilt my head as I huff in a steady breath. He's gazing back at me with the same need in his eyes that he had when he was on his knees in front of me. The same desire, silently telling me how much he wanted me.

I can't help but dip my eyes to his crotch, the bulge in his pants has softened with the turn of events but I can still see the outline of his cock pushing through the thin fabric of his pants. A flood of emotions runs through me.

I was ready to return the favor and get on my knees for him. Wanting to experience what it was like to suck another man's cock. But not just any man's, his. The only man I've ever seen in another light other than platonic friendship. The only guy I've ever been attracted to.

Jasper shifts his stance feeling my lingering gaze. Shaking my head, I stare at the floor with so many thoughts and so much confusion.

"I know you want to explore this, Wade. You want Abby and whatever she and Major are bringing into this mix." He swallows audibly. "You want me. You want all of this, just as much as I do."

"I don't want to make anything harder for Lily." I admit to him because kids have it rough these days. I would never want her to feel ashamed if other kids made fun of her for something I choose in my life.

"Who cares if she has two dads or ten. As long as she's taken care of, loved and first priority, that other shit doesn't matter,

Wade. Kids are going to be kids—people are going to be people —regardless of your sexual orientation."

He doesn't get it. I don't want her to feel like she needs to justify my choices. She's going to have to learn to stand up for herself, I don't need her to have to stand up for me, too. I've seen it with people these days, the judgment. I'm just not ready for all that.

I continue to shake my head back and forth like it's stuck on a loop. "Just…get out of my way." I'm defeated, lost for words, but I stand tall again and look him dead in the eyes.

He huffs out a breath, his lips press into a tight frown as his eyes trail up and down my body before he meets my gaze. It looks like he wants to say something, but pauses then steps to the side.

I pass him and rush out, turning the corner of the hallway into the garage, coming to a dead stop in the doorway of the living area.

Major glances up at me from the island as he hands a box of Cheerios to my sister, then his eyes shift over to where Abby and Lily are sitting.

It looks like they've been playing with some toys, pulling some of the donated items out of a box.

Abby's legs are criss-crossed on the floor next to the coffee table and she has a doll in her hands. Lily's eyes are engaged and bouncing between Abby and the doll with adorable curiosity.

"Binky," Lily says, pointing at the pacifier in its mouth.

"Yeah, she's got one just like you," Abby says with a smile as she taps gently on the one that's in Lily's mouth.

"Wade has been trying to wean her off that pacifier for the past year but it's the only thing that keeps her calm so it's been really tough." My sister shares with Abby as she gives Lily an incredulous look.

Lily knows that look and peers up at her with puppy dog eyes then says, "mine."

"That look right there, wins us over every time," Rachel says as Abby giggles.

"I can understand why," she agrees.

"There's actually a story behind little miss Daisy here." Abby shows Lily the doll and I recognize it as the same cabbage patch kid that I saw in the box she carried in when she arrived.

"A brave little girl gave this to me. She told me she was once lost at a fire station and Daisy was there when she got there." My heart drops as Abby continues the story. "She said Daisy made her feel not so alone." She hands Lily the doll and her eyes light up. A bright smile beams over her face and it's contagious, going viral between all of us as we mirror her smile.

"The little girl and Daisy left the fire station and found a home with a nice family. They were the best of friends, but now that the little girl is all grown up she said she wanted to give it back to the fire station so Daisy could take care of another little girl. Maybe Daisy is here to help you." Abby pulls the pacifier out of the doll's mouth and sets in on the table next to them. Lily mocks the movement by taking out hers and setting it next to the one on the table, but quickly puts the binky back in her mouth and does the same to the doll, then pulls it into her arms.

We all laugh at her possessive gesture over both the doll and the binky. The fact that she took it out and matched the movement was actually a huge step and tells me she completely understands.

I know what Abby is saying even though the story is modified for my three-year-old. It breaks my heart whenever I hear stories like that because there are so many *what if's* that could have happened to my daughter.

"Was that little girl a safe surrender?" my sister asks.

Abby turns to look at my sister and nods sadly.

"Just like Lily," Rachel replies with an annoyed tone because she hated my ex and views her solely as an egg donor. Also, I need to remind my sister to tighten her non-existent filter later.

I glance over at Abby, her brows knit together as she glances back at me. A million questions running through those beautiful, rich brown eyes of hers.

"My ex, she dropped her off here, but she was too much of a coward to confront me and left her outside under the safe surrender sign."

Her mouth opens but nothing comes out. She peers down at Lily then back up at me, a pissed off expression crosses her face before she covers it up and smiles.

"Well then, it's perfect isn't it? Daisy and Lily, two little beauties that can bloom together." She taps Lily on the nose and they scrunch up their noses at the same time.

Well, fuck that's adorable and suddenly all the anxiety from a few minutes ago is gone and replaced with a sense of happiness I can't quite describe.

I run in a constant state of worry with too many demands and guilt, mostly from myself, that I'm not doing enough for her. Yet, I glance around the room at my sister who helps take care of her when I'm working. At Major, who treats her like a kid of his own, buying her more presents than I do, spoiling her to the ends of the Earth.

Then to Abby. Someone I hardly know, yet Lily's already smitten with her as easily as we are.

Even Jasper, who hasn't come into the room yet, is the literal definition of a 'Funcle' and Lily laughs every time he's in the room. They've taken her, and me, in like family.

We are family.

And now I'm fucking pissed at myself for how I over-reacted with Jasper back in the room. Guilt blankets me as I glance over my shoulder looking for him but he's nowhere to be seen.

"What are you wearing?" my sister asks with a tad too much judgment in her tone, as she places a small bowl of cheerios on the table next to Lily and walks toward me.

I glance down, inspecting myself and huff out an annoyed chuckle. Jasper didn't even fucking say anything.

"Aren't those Jasper's clothes?" she adds, as Major and Abby turn to look in my direction in harmonious motion, chuckling as they take in my mismatched attire.

My sweats I thought I put on are actually Jasper's skinny joggers, if that's even a thing. They fit far too snug around my tree trunks for legs and the shirt, well shit. I roll my eyes as I read the words, *MOUNTAINS AREN'T FUNNY, THEY ARE HILL AREAS*.

A vintage drawing of a mountain sits in the middle in between and it's just *so* Jasper.

It's also a size too small, which makes sense why I could hardly pull it over my head. I was just so flustered I wasn't even thinking straight.

I'm still not thinking straight after everything that's happened. And my sister, who has zero filter and suffers from verbal diarrhea disorder, can't help herself.

"You look thoroughly," she lowers her voice to a whisper so Lily doesn't hear, "fucked." She stops in front of me, brushing her fingers through my hair attempting to tame it, but then rubs her fingertips into my scalp messing it up even more. "Did you wrestle Jasper and lose?" She laughs as she pulls at the hem of the shirt that rests just above the waistband of these tiny joggers.

"Knock it off." I tip my head back as I slap her hand away. Unfortunately, she knows me way too well and reads me like a book.

"What's up with you?" she asks as she glances over her shoulder looking at Abby, then back to me. "A mystery girl is here, you're dressed in Jasper's clothes, and Major is being weird."

"Nothing," I say too quickly to not be obvious. I avert my gaze and slow my words, trying to recover from looking guilty.

"I was just in the shower, heard you guys come in and dressed in the first thing I could find."

"Sorry, I'm late," Jasper strides in the room with his usual confidence, "I was in the shower." He kisses my speechless sister on the cheek then bounces over to Lily picking her up, swinging her around before bringing her in for a hug.

Rachel hums, giving me a calculated look and I palm my face.

Jesus fucking christ.

"It's not what it looks like," is all I can manage to say.

She hums again, this time her eyebrows raise in a slightly disappointed way. "Well, that's a bummer. I hoped it was."

I go to open my mouth to rebuttal, say something back, anything, but I can't find the words. She steps away, heading over to sit with Lily, Jasper and Abby.

Has everyone known my annoyance with Jasper was always a crush? I didn't even realize it myself at first. How could they?

Sure, I figured Major would know, being that he worked with us day in and day out, but others. No way.

Right?

I shake away my confused thoughts and walk toward Lily. She's still in Jasper's arms but reaches out for me when I get closer. I can't help the ear-to-ear grin that crosses over my face as I reach back.

"Hey, baby girl." I intentionally brush my hand softly over Jasper's as I pull her into me. Like I'm offering an olive branch, a silent apology for my stupid over-reaction. My eyes shift in his direction but he quickly pulls away, avoiding my gaze as he squats down next to Abby.

"Look, I got a doll," Lily says, holding it up.

I inspect the tattered thing, cringing internally, but still manage to smile at her, "She's beautiful, just like you," I say, kissing her forehead.

"Are we all staying for dinner?" Major asks as he sorts some vegetables on the kitchen island.

Geez. Is it already time for dinner? I glance over at the clock, shocked to see it's well past 7:00 p.m. and close to Lily's bedtime.

"I've got to get Lily home for a bath and bedtime so we can be up early for Santa Claus," Rachel singsongs walking back over to us.

A disappointed look must pass over my face as my sister gives me a tight-lipped smile.

She just got here with Lily and I haven't had any time with her tonight. The thought that I won't get to tuck Lily in on Christmas Eve is like a guilt laced anchor weighing on my heart. But it was either that or work on Christmas day and we all decided this was better than the latter. And it is, but our shift switch doesn't happen until 7:00 a.m. I just hope I make it home before Lily wakes up.

I kiss my baby girl and Rachel says her goodbyes making insinuating, inappropriate comments. Like, *stay outta trouble you four,* with a knowing tone, and *work hard, play hard,* with a wink to Major, like she suspects what's happening between us.

Which…who knows. I don't even know what's happening between all of us.

With Lily in tow I watch Rachel leave and think to myself how grateful I am for her and everything she does for me and Lily. I honestly have no idea what I would do without her.

"I should probably head out, too," Abby says and we all turn in her direction. Simultaneously our rebuttals overlap each other.

"No," Major demands.

"No, uh uh," Jasper whines.

"Don't go," I plead.

Her arms fly up in defense with a surprised look on her face that morphs quickly into a shy smile as a blush crosses her cheeks. I have to smother my own smile seeing how cute her reaction is to all of our neediness.

It's a stark contrast from the woman we pleased less than an hour ago and I'm drawn to both versions of her equally.

"Okay, but only for dinner. Then I need to go," she insists as she looks around the room at us. We all silently agree, reluctantly. Then she squeals as Jasper pulls her into his lap.

My eyes lock on hers as Jasper nuzzles into her neck and yet another displeased look crosses my face because it's a sharp reality that what we're doing here is temporary.

CHAPTER 33
FOUR-GONE CONCLUSION

MAJOR

Abby's fucking perfect.

And I mean that in all the ways it can be meant.

She's gorgeous, kind, unbelievably sexy and she matches with all three of us in different ways. It's like a portion of her soul was created for each of us.

I internally cringe at my sappiness because that sounds cliché, but it's the truth.

Is it possible to meet your perfect match and know she's not *just* for you? I've been around a lot longer than all of them. I know exactly what I want and what makes sense for me. I knew I would never remarry. I enjoyed marriage for what it was, but I also knew that it wasn't for me. It didn't have anything to do with committing to another person. I'm without a doubt loyal and committed in anything that I'm passionate about, but my likes and dislikes are too particular and what makes sense for me would probably not make sense for others.

But with these three, something just clicks. Physically, emotionally, sexually.

Now, if I can just get Wade to see it.

The moment he heard Rachel's voice, he kicked Jasper away so fast, I swear it was like he thought he was a bomb waiting to explode.

I'm actually surprised at how well Jasper is acting. Well, maybe not. Jasper takes everything in stride. But I can't imagine how vulnerable he felt when Wade did that.

He seems to be okay now but he's also using Abby as a shield, holding on to her like he wants to trap her in his arms and never let go.

She's smiling and asking questions as they cuddle on the couch talking about his family farm and their first meeting at the Farmer's Market. I love how relaxed they feel together.

"They're good together," Wade says as he steps up next to me, placing the cutting board on the counter.

His body is rigid, rivaling the intensity of his gaze on them, contradicting the easiness in his words and I see exactly what he's doing. Pushing her, us, away before he gets hurt.

"We're all good together," I reply as I turn toward him and lean into the kitchen island. I can tell he wants to say more. He wants to say a lot. I think he normally does but he keeps to himself, holding back all the things he wants to say and do for fear of what, I don't know.

"Lily's getting big," I change the subject because I know this will get him talking.

He smiles, that adoring smile only a smitten father can have. "She is, she's talking a lot. Understanding so much more every-day. Scary as hell."

"She'll be understanding about a lot of things, you know," I add and he just nods slowly as he chops the carrots I left out on the counter.

"She'll understand your schedule is challenging, working the shifts we work. She'll understand that you do this to give her a good life with as many opportunities as possible. And she'll understand if you start dating someone, *anyone*," I pronounce slowly, deliberately, "male, female…multiple," I add.

He stops chopping and side-eyes me, then looks down taking a deep breath through his nose.

His eyes shut, like he's talking himself into speaking and when he reopens them they're laser focused on Jasper and Abby.

"What the hell does that even look like Major? I've never even had a healthy relationship with one woman, how could I even manage being good enough for her, for…us."

"I've had multiple relationships that have ended in a break up and one massively failed marriage. I'm definitely not the right person to answer that question," I say, honestly.

His shoulders are still tense and his face screws up as he glares at me.

"If you're trying to sell me on this whole poly thing, you're failing miserably."

I chuckle, because it's not often that Wade has a snarky come back. Jasper is rubbing off on him in a good way.

"No, what I'm saying is I haven't had the best run with women and neither have you. Jasper has had a ton of surface level relationships but nothing serious because, honestly, I don't think one person will ever be able to satisfy him. We're all still single and we're enjoying this. I don't see why we can't figure it out…talk about it. See if it will work, you know?" I glance over at him and I can see he's absorbing my words even though he's completely silent. "There's a strong connection we all have with Abby. You and Jasper are…" He winces as he frowns and I can tell it's not from disgust but from shame. And I don't know if it's because he likes Jasper and doesn't know how to process it or feels bad for how he treated him. I skim over that and avoid elaborating my thoughts on that. "And me, well, you know my situation. It's a good fit," I state, factually.

He pauses for a moment then shakes his head.

"I don't know, Maj. I just—"

Wade is interrupted by the incessant buzzing of Abby's phone that's on the corner of the coffee table. It's already buzzed once, which by way of modern day default we all easily ignored. But as it continues, the microscopic but continuous movement now places the phone at the edge of the table and it's on the verge of falling off.

Just as Abby glances in its direction, it takes the dive off the table and hits the floor with a resounding thud. Jasper reaches out for it from his spot on the couch, his body still wrapped around Abby, and she giggles as he squeaks out a grunt, his fingertips finding the corner of the phone case and finally takes a hold of it.

He passes it to Abby only after making her give him a kiss for it.

Wade rolls his eyes, but I don't miss the corner of his mouth turning up ever so slightly at their adorable behavior.

Although I keep my eye on Abby because as I've seen so far, she's got a lot of so-called friends that aren't really friends, and I'm wondering if it's the same person who called to cancel on her earlier.

She was so disappointed after getting off that call, and when she told me why, I completely understood. No one as young as her should be alone on Christmas. She shouldn't be alone ever, but during the holidays, that's ludicrous in my opinion. So, for her *friend* to cancel on her, well, that doesn't seem like much of a friend to me.

I watch as she taps on her phone, her brows pinch together and her expression slowly morphs from happy to confused, a concerned look crosses her face, then her face falls as her eyes skim back and forth over the screen.

Jasper is none the wiser, since he's laying behind her, mindlessly twirling a piece of her hair in his finger. She must tense because he stops, glances over her shoulder and peers at her phone. He looks dumbfounded and slightly confused. He cranes his neck forward, trying to get a good look at her face, as if to check on her well-being.

She sits up urgently, and now I can't help but ask, "What's wrong, Abby?"

CHAPTER 34
ALL GOOD THINGS COME TO AN END

ABBY

> Sam: I'm calling you, pick up. I need to explain.

> Cami: Hey…please call me.

> Sam: Don't ignore me.

> Sam: Sienna is crazy. Don't listen to her. It's always been you, baby.

> Cami: Why aren't you picking up?

To say I'm confused is an understatement.

I know he's been seeing Sienna since I caught them in bed together. Even though he tells me *it was a one time thing.* He tries his best to hide it because he wants people to think he's still dating that, and I quote, *'hot influencer with a million followers.'* He's been desperately trying so hard to get back with me so he hasn't been publicly dating anyone, but I know he's still seeing Sienna.

I have no idea why he continues to try. He's a lying, manipulating cheat and I would have to be out of my goddamn mind to even consider such a thing.

He treated me like shit, used me, and then cheated on me. I'm so done.

I don't care much about what he has to say, but Cami's text is concerning.

As I click on her name to respond to ask what is going on, a message from Sienna pulls down on the top banner of my phone. My heart rate spikes and I can't help but instantly tap to open the message.

Sienna: I'm tired of being his dirty little secret.

Sienna: socialshare.com/siennastylesyou/1kpgl2

Oh, god. Oh, no. I don't know what she's posted but what if she got a hold of something that I don't want public. It's not like I did anything scandalous with Sam but what if he recorded something without me knowing about it that Sienna found. Sadly, I wouldn't put that past either one of them.

My breath stalls in my throat and my heart beats wildly out of control as I click on the link.

A video pops up from Sienna's social media with a shaky recording of a dark screen. There's no sound, just static scratchiness overlapping heavy breathing and footsteps clacking in the background. Like heels on concrete.

A sliver of light from a distance highlights the outline of a car then suddenly, a bright light flashes on the screen, the auto-focus overcorrects itself with the harsh contrast. I even squint adjusting to the brightness.

"You fucking asshole!" Sienna shrieks as her hand flails forward over the screen, nailing a man in the back of his head. The screen is shaking but I can easily make out Sam's profile as he pulls his arms over his head to protect himself.

"Sienna, stop. Jesus. It's not what it looks like!" he screams. Deja vu, because I've heard that before.

She doesn't stop smacking him as she continues to spit out profanities and names at him. It looks like he was truly caught off guard and at this point can only defend himself by covering himself and the woman he's laying on top of.

I breathe out a small chuckle at the sight because, well, karma.

"Sienna, stop!" the other girl screams out.

"I know you were sneaking behind my back, you slut!"

Sienna stops hitting Sam and her camera focuses on the girl laying topless underneath Sam. Her arms are crossed over each other to cover her breasts as she peers up into the camera.

"Oh my god," my hand covers my mouth as my voice cracks even though my words are barely a whisper.

Cami.

"Are you recording this?" Cami shrieks as she squints, her eyes bouncing between the screen and Sienna standing behind it.

"You're damn right I am, and you know exactly where it's going." Cami pushes Sam off and sits up just as the screen cuts off and the video ends.

"Cami—" I cut myself off because it's all the words I can muster. I'm frozen in this position. Staring at the blank screen dumbfounded, shocked, disappointed, and completely heartbroken.

That was Cami. My best friend. The person I would confide in the most. The same girl that spent the holidays with me. The same girl that stood next to me during my mother's funeral.

I drop my phone to the ground as Major rushes up to the right side of me, while Jasper consoles me from my left side. Dipping my head into my open palms, I cover my face because I don't want them to see the tears in my eyes and the shame on my face.

I didn't make my break up with Sam known because I was trying to maintain some privacy. Now I realize how stupid that was because everyone just found out he wasn't just cheating on me with Sienna but it appears with Cami, too. My two closest friends.

My phone starts pinging incessantly and I can see the notifications popping up from the screen. I'm getting tagged nonstop in the video, it's being shared and reposted. Alert after alert after alert. It scrolls up over the screen like credits at the end of a movie.

How fucking embarassing.

I could care less about Sam at this point. Sienna can get trapped in a traveling porta potty for all I care, but Cami. Cami's betrayal wrecks me.

"He's not worth it, pumpkin," Jasper whispers to me as he kisses my temple. I don't have the energy to explain how little I care about Sam and what he did. I actually don't even care that it's shared all over social media. I'm used to my life being public and people saying whatever shit they feel like spewing out about me at any given moment.

I can be the most beautiful, kindest woman one second and if I promote or dislike something they don't, I instantly become the villain in their life story. It's like my opinion was a personal attack against them.

Even if I wear the wrong thing that doesn't flatter my body type or if I'm wearing a warm tone versus a cool tone that doesn't compliment my skin type. They have more than enough to say about their opinions on how I look or what I do.

My skin has grown thick over the past year and fortunately I've learned how to move past it.

But this is a level of drama I don't feel like dealing with. Not when I feel grief and mourning from the loss of someone who I thought was a true friend.

"Was that the same Cami you were talking to earlier?" Major asks, and of course he does, because he pays attention to every minute detail. Jasper's body tenses next to mine and somehow I find it in me to nod.

"I see," he says as he glances at Jasper, then back over to Wade.

Wade hasn't moved from his spot behind the kitchen island. He's just been watching the three of us and I don't know if it's because he knows I have Jasper and Major here or if he's uncomfortable with crying women but I feel like I need them all.

I glance in his direction, silently asking for his comfort, too, but he doesn't move. He stands there like an iceberg, stuck in the same spot and stoic as hell.

He was so kind to me in his room earlier today when it was just the two of us. During our Truth or Dare and Guess Who game he was adventurous and brave but now, he's the same cold Wade that answered the door when I first arrived. His scowl has returned and as much as I don't care about other people's opinions, I really care what he's thinking.

And that grates on my nerves.

It's natural to lean on someone you feel close to in a time of need but as I look at these three men staring back at me I realize I've done that far too often in my life. And look where it has gotten me.

My trust issues are hitting hard.

I'm not sure if it's the video I just saw, the betrayal I feel, or me just trying to sabotage everything in my life but I can't handle Wade's judgmental gaze. The embarrassment of this happening in front of them is devastating and mortifying.

So what do we do when trying to handle emotions we don't understand, but can't manage to control because of the overwhelming sensation of humiliation, uncontrollably lash out.

"What is your problem?" I stand, staring straight at him. His eyes widen and trail up with me as I rise to my full height. "Are you judging me? Do you want to tell me how stupid I am? Make fun of me like a million other people are right now?" His look is a mix of confusion and pity, as he shakes his head, but he remains silent, not fighting for me, not saying anything, and that pisses me off even more.

"Abby—" Major's hand wraps gently around my elbow. His voice is soft and assuring as he attempts to calm me down but I hate how impersonal my real name sounds coming from his mouth with that tone.

"This was a mistake. Staying here was a mistake," I say as I bend down to grab my phone. I'm being completely irrational. I know I am. The normally level-headed Abby is screaming at me from one side but the completely unreasonable, devastatingly heartbroken Abby is taking the wheel and there's no stopping her.

"Abby, it's not a mis—" Jasper stands, taking a step toward me but I put my hand up stopping him from continuing to move or talk. Even Jasper's kind tone sounds harsh to my sensitive ears.

I can't do this. I need to form the words. I need to say them out loud because it's the only way this won't end up with me even more broken than I already feel. I can barely handle a relationship with one person, much less three. And what are they going to do, share me?

"This was never going to work." I manage to spit out the words and they feel like razor blades on my lips. I hate it, because I know it was more than just sex. There was a connection. A desire we all shared. But I'm thinking too much with my broken heart to do anything that will continue to hurt me.

Major steps forward with purpose, his body language is demanding and I expect the same with his words but as he goes to open his mouth an ear splitting ringing blares through the station.

I have to bow my head and cover my ears as the deafening sound pierces my ears. The shrieking sound of the fire alarm bounces off the cement walls and echoes through every room in the station.

The guys all look at each other and Wade is the first to react, diving around the kitchen island and racing toward the lockers in the garage.

"Goddamn it." Major runs his hands through his hair, then steps toward me. "Stay here, please stay here." His eyes beg along with his words. I return a dispirited look and he frowns as he steps back because he knows.

He knows I won't stay.

"Fuck," Major spits out. A single word laced with so much mixed emotion. Frustration, hurt, anger. "Jasper, let's go. Now." He takes a giant leap back then turns, running into the garage behind Wade.

"No!" Jasper screams back at Major as he grabs my hands. "This can work, we will work."

I can't have him touch me right now. I can't get pulled into this orbit I've been in with him, with them. His touch is soft and inviting and as much as I wanted that a few minutes ago, I need to protect myself. I pull my hands away and avoid his gaze. "You have to go, Jasper."

"Abby, please."

There he goes with *Abby*, too. These men have spoiled me with my nicknames so much that now I despise my real one.

"You have to go." I pin him with a look that says I'm serious.

I have literally been saved by the bell and need to take full advantage of it. This is the perfect excuse to leave with no ties, nothing. "Go!"

Wade runs past the open doorway completely dressed in his gear, screaming for Jasper as the garage door opens. "We can't stay for her, Jasper. We have to leave, right now!"

"Wade's right," I reply to Jasper.

Wade's always been right. He's been the stand-offish one. The one that makes the right judgment calls and thinks with more logic than heart, which is exactly what I need to do.

Jasper's eyes squeeze shut, as if in pain then turns around, running into the garage with more speed than both of the others combined.

The truck's engine roars to life as Major runs to the passenger side and it begins to inch its way out of the garage. Jasper flies by jumping onto the back of the moving truck, pinning me with one last look. It's full of sadness and a silent plea, but it's useless because today is over. It's come to an end like it was always meant to.

I already feel so hurt and I have no interest in damaging myself any further.

And by the pained look he returns back at me, he knows it too.

CHAPTER 35
I SUCK AT APOLOGIES, SO UNFUCK YOU OR WHATEVER

WADE - ONE WEEK LATER

I walk through the doors of the station with my duffle bag draped over my shoulder. I pause looking through the doorway into the kitchen to see if Major or Jasper have arrived yet, but as usual, I'm the first one here for our shift.

I two-finger wave at Roy and he tips his chin at me as I continue walking toward my room. He covered for me earlier in the week so I really owe him one.

Lily woke up with a fever the day after Christmas and even though she looked like she was feeling fine, I didn't feel comfortable leaving her with Rachel.

Honestly, I just wasn't ready to come in and face either one of the guys, so I called out and Roy stepped in to cover.

Apparently Jasper called out as well and Major had no issues texting us telling us to stop being babies and avoiding our *issues*.

Other than that group text chain, I haven't talked to either one of them since Christmas Eve.

I'm prepared for today to be awkward as fuck with what happened between all of us, especially between me and Jasper.

On Christmas morning, we all returned to the station with a sliver of hope that she could be there. We remained silent when we pulled up to the station and that signature mint green Ford Bronco of hers was gone.

The only evidence signifying everything was real was the bandana that was still splayed out on the floor as we parked the truck.

Still, we all walked into the break room, silently praying she would still be there, but she was really gone.

I stared at the couch where she sat when she found out her friends and ex betrayed her and my heart broke for her again. I hated the last moments with her, when she thought I didn't care about her or how she was feeling. Because that wasn't the case at all. It was a sense of de-ja-vu for me. My ex left me with our daughter and ran off with my best friend. The words were there on the tip of my tongue to tell her she wasn't alone, but I froze. I didn't know how to comfort her or what to do and I hated how strong my feelings were for someone I just met.

So, instead of confronting those feelings and sharing my past, I remained quiet and reserved so she just assumed I was being a prick. Then that goddamn fire alarm went off and I ran out of here like this was the room that was on fire. I'm disgusted with myself with how I acted, how I treated her.

The fire we got called to that night was a Class C electrical fire in a large commercial building. Fortunately the building was empty since it was a holiday, but we couldn't extinguish it by customary methods and it took longer for us to put it out. By the time we finished and got back it was well after ten in the morning. So, naturally I ignored any conversation that could have been brought up and snatched up the Lego fire truck that Abby and I built then went home as quickly as I could. Lily was happily playing with Daisy, the cabbage patch doll Abby gave her and her new obsession.

I was shocked to find she wasn't sucking on the pacifier that she relies on so much because she said she's a big girl who needs to take care of Daisy and big girls don't need pacifiers.

Then asked where Abby was.

My daughter was just as smitten with Abby, too.

Can't say I blame her.

The level of exhaustion I felt after the day and night we had was easily ignored by the smile plastered on my baby girl's face as she opened all her presents. It was the first year she really understood who Santa Claus is and that Christmas day equates to presents. Her excitement was contagious.

For the first time, I felt bothered that we didn't have someone to share it with. You would think I would daydream about what it would be like to have Lily's mom in the picture, to be the happy family we were supposed to be. But, instead my thoughts trailed back to Abby, Jasper, and Major. Because that's who feels like family to me.

I've had a week to overthink what happened on Christmas Eve and dissect my relationship with Major and Jasper. I feel like I've spent every minute of this past week pondering the what if's and possible scenarios.

I've always had a strong, reliable relationship with Major and Jasper. Even though Jasper and I had our issues, the three of us have always been stronger together than we were apart. Our relationship was always platonic, never sexual, but Abby changed that. She brought out what Jasper and I were suppressing for so long and I've finally come to accept it for what it is.

I want us to be more than friends but I also want Abby, and what Major brings. Because, somehow for some reason, when it was the four of us, it felt complete.

It's totally unconventional but somehow I always end at the conclusion that a four-way relationship between all of us is worth exploring.

And after a week-long come-to-Jesus talk with myself, I'm confident walking into the station today to tell Major and Jasper that.

It's New Year's Eve and I'm ready to make a permanent resolution for all of us.

CHAPTER 36
IS THERE A 12-STEP PROGRAM FOR LOVE ADDICTS?

JASPER

This is the first day I've ever walked into this station with a feeling of dread. I've never let other people's emotions or thoughts change my behavior or drive my actions but for some reason I can't let go of what happened last week.

Abby opened something up in all of us that was dormant and her presence was like a volcanic eruption that was doomed to happen.

I'm not the type of person to typically feel regret and I still don't, I think.

No, I know I don't. I don't regret what happened. But I'm terrified of the unknown, of how Wade will respond to me now that it has happened.

I'm fearful of the consequences. But I guess that's what true regret is, right?

You never feel the heaviness of your decisions, unless you don't like the outcome.

I'm going to plaster on the face that I've perfected over the years and pretend like nothing happened. Like he didn't push me away, literally kicking me while I was down in the most compromising position, because that's what's best right now.

If I've come to learn anything about Wade, it's how he'll just completely ignore an emotional confrontation to avoid conflict.

And, I accept it because it's part of who he is.

Usually I stop to say hi to everyone when I first walk in, but I'm not in the mood today, so I pass by the break room and head straight to the room that I've shared with Wade for so many years.

I'm not surprised when I walk through the doorway to see him unpacking the clothes from his duffle bag. He's always the first one here, but I still say, "Oh, hey, you're here," like it's not normal.

He visibly stiffens as he drops his arms to his side and I'm preparing myself for the same anger and frustration he normally spits back at me.

Lay it on me, Wade. I won't fight back with you anymore. I'm too in love with you now.

I silently admit the confession to myself.

Then proceed with the internal introduction to my own 12 step program.

Hi, my name is Jasper and I fell in love with three people on Christmas Eve. Nothing will ever make me feel whole again and I'm just trying to survive.

Hi, Jasper. I cheer myself on.

Wade finally turns around with a frown I don't recognize.

He takes one step in my direction, then another long stride and I brace myself, squinting one eye shut as I dip my chin away.

Instead of a brute fist to my face, I'm shocked when he grabs my neck and pulls my face into his, planting his lips against mine.

What. The. Fuck.

I question it, but for only a millisecond because the moment his hot tongue sweeps over mine I moan and melt straight into him. Pretty much forgiving him instantly.

He kisses me like it means something to him. His touch is full of conviction, unlike the Truth or Dare kiss we had. That was amazing, don't get me wrong. But his body reacted to me with more anxiety and nerves than with lust.

This…this is pure need. Like his body needs this to survive.

"Holy shit," I breathe out as he pulls away. Sucking in a deep breath, I try calming my racing pulse after that unbelievably mind blowing kiss. "I was not expecting that. I thought you were going to punch me."

"I thought about it," he bounces his head back and forth, "there was like a fifty-fifty chance." He pauses, his throat bobs as he swallows thickly. "but then I saw you and couldn't help myself." A rare, shy smile graces his face and damn, it's a priceless sight.

"Well…I *am* charming, you know. Impossible to resist. It's a known fact," I joke playfully, because I already know how hard that was for him to admit, and this will be better…for now.

He steps back, running his hand through his thick, wavy hair. He turns his gaze away, with a slight look of shame, before focusing back on me again. "I'm sorry, Jasper. I didn't understand my feelings and I treated you like shit, and I'm sorry." Genuine remorse laces his tone and I hate how hard he's being on himself.

If anyone can relate to not knowing what to do with mixed feelings about the same gender, it's me.

I want him to know that it's okay and I forgive him but I also need him to know exactly how I feel about him, about what happened and he needs to know how serious I am.

"I understand why you reacted the way you did and it's okay." I tilt my head to reach his gaze that still peers toward the ground. "I get it, I really do. But, I need you to know that this isn't just a fling for me. I want this," I gesture my finger between the two of us, "and I don't want to give up on the idea of all of us. What happened on Christmas Eve—"

"I want that, too," he interrupts. "All of it. I have no idea what it looks like or how it's going to work, but I want to try."

"Well, I'm glad that's out of the way," Major chimes in, surprising us both.

His arms are crossed, one leg over the other as he leans in the doorway like he's been planted there for a decade, comfortable and smug.

Voyeuristic bastard.

"How long have you been there?" I furrow my brow.

"Long enough." He smiles, as he pushes himself off the wall and steps into the room with us.

It feels like how it's always felt. Like we're a cohesive team, who respect each other, but there is a deeper, more meaningful connection now, there's just one important piece missing.

"Are we going to do this?" Major asks, as he looks between us.

I glance at Wade as he side-eyes me and our knowing smiles mirror each other.

"Hell yeah," I reply at the same time Wade nods with a rare smile.

"Good. Let's go get our girl."

CHAPTER 37
QUADRUPLE THE FUN

ABBY

"Hey guys! *BayAreaAbby* checking in at the farmer's market. Today I'm hanging out with the amazing team at the Healthy Horizons booth," I aim the camera toward Rayna and Mark as they wave, "We're chatting about our resolutions and how to create better habits in the New Year. Come by and say hi!" I tap the stop recording button and post it with less enthusiasm than normal.

It's the first post I've made since the donation video at the fire station. In fact, this is the first one on my new phone.

After I left the fire station, I drove straight home with tear puddled eyes after the emotional overload and mass regret.

At the time I had no idea what the regret was for. My joke of a relationship with Sam, Cami's betrayal, or pushing away three amazing men for fear of getting hurt even more.

By the time I walked through my door I knew it was all of the above, but that Christmas Eve experience carried the most weight.

I didn't regret getting involved with them. They treated me like a princess. A frown pierces my lips with the thought of

Major's nickname for me. Something about him just exudes strength and when I was alone on Christmas Eve, I missed his comforting presence. I craved the playful banter I had with Jasper and the bond I made with Wade.

I scolded myself for how I acted, lashing out on them for no goddamn reason. I just couldn't even see straight after what Cami did, and my guttural reaction to that betrayal caused me to lose more friendships in my life.

Still, I needed space. I needed time. I needed to distance myself.

I should have posted something, explained that I wasn't with Sam anymore—that I hadn't been for quite some time. But every time I thought about saying something, it didn't feel right, because I felt like I was defending myself for *their* actions.

So, instead, I shut off my phone and ignored social media for the week.

Who am I kidding? I ignored life for a week.

It was actually quite liberating. The peace. The quiet. Not finding reasons, a purpose to post something, anything, for content.

Sure, I vegged out on too much junk food, watched really bad reality tv, and I think the odds of getting the same delivery driver from an app service—three times, by the way—is about the same as winning the lottery.

But, I needed that disconnect.

After the week-long hiatus was over I felt like I needed a fresh start without the distraction of Cami or Sam. So, yesterday I forced myself out of the house and purchased a new phone, changing my phone number for the first time in my life.

I've had the same number since my mom got me a cell phone when I was thirteen years old. When the sales guy asked if I wanted to transfer over my contacts, text messages, photos and apps, I told him contacts and photos only, but immediately went in and blocked the numbers for Sam, Sienna, and Cami, then deleted their information.

As I removed the *'Cheating Bastard'* contact, the next name that popped up was: Dad.

My heart broke a little. Wondering if it was silly that I still kept it in my phone as contacts even though I know I'll never see that name pop up on my screen again.

I left it anyway because it feels like a comfort having it in there.

Like a true clean slate, I had no texts in my messages app and was required to download the apps I needed on this phone. I only downloaded the ones I needed, which was really nice because I didn't use ninety percent of the apps I had on my old phone.

It felt cleansing.

The only thing that continued to preoccupy my thoughts was *them*. I wanted to go see them multiple times, but talked myself out of it.

And for good reason.

Because a majority of the solo time I had was much needed and I spent all of that time teaching myself how to be better at being alone. I never thought I had an issue with this until I felt like I truly had no one. Including the million people behind the small screen of my phone. I've used those virtual, and practically faceless, relationships more than I should have because if I wasn't talking to someone, I felt like I was living my life in solitary. In reality, I just never knew how to enjoy the solo version of me.

I needed to find enjoyment in myself.

And honestly, it felt good.

Admittedly though, the other portion of my time was spent dissecting all the ways something could possibly work between me, Major, Wade, and Jasper. Because no matter how hard I tried to push that thought away, I couldn't. They embedded themselves in me so easily, so quickly, and I conjured up all the ways that it could make sense.

I want it to make sense.

I know I need to start by apologizing for my actions and how I reacted toward them, but I couldn't muster the courage to just show up at the station.

Plus, I have no idea when they work or what their schedule is and my emotional state last week couldn't handle being rejected, even if it was because of a simple fact of them not being there.

So, I decided I need a grand gesture. I need to find a way to apologize—profusely—tell them how I feel, and manifest what I want.

I find myself peering over in the direction of Jasper's family pop up, but I don't see it here today. The spot it's normally at has a table with fresh honeycomb and honey jarring tools.

"So, how're you holding up?" Rayna asks, as she places brochures on the table.

Her tone is kind. But I still have a hard time wondering who's asking for purposes of checking in on my well-being and who's asking to hear the inside scoop of all the drama.

"Oh, that's last week's news." I wave my hand like it's no big deal. Which is partially true. There's so much hype when it first happens, but fades immediately with the next jaw-dropping gossip event. "Sam and I broke up over a month ago and I already knew about his, you know, side activities." I didn't know about Cami but I leave it vague because I don't really want to talk about it. She senses it and changes the topic.

"Well, those firefighters you interviewed last week were… wow," she says as she fans herself. "Oh, how I'd love to be trapped in a building with them."

Yeah, I guess that's probably a normal reaction. I mean, I can't say I didn't feel the same way the moment I met them. Even so, a wave of possessiveness floats over me and I can't help but want to rip her fingernails out of her nail beds for talking about my guys in such a suggestive way.

Oh, god. Listen to me.

My guys.

Claiming them like Tarzan. I'm not normally a jealous person but thinking about them with other people drives me to the brink of madness.

Fuck it. I'm going to go to the station…now.

"You know, I have to—"

"Oh my god. Is that them?" She hits my arm with the top of her hand then points in the direction of the pedestrian entrance of the market.

I whiplash my neck in that direction to see a small fire truck parking in the fire lane at the front entrance. The doors open in unison as my three gorgeous men step out of the truck and I swear it plays out in my head like the best slow motion video ever made.

Major stands in between the two of them, leading the stride with his commanding presence. His dark hair is freshly cut, the salt and pepper sides are evenly trimmed, and the short stubble that decorates his face looks delicious on him. He has a barely there smile and, in true Major fashion, his eyes lock on mine like I'm the only one he sees.

Jasper's normally shaggy hair is pulled back showing his intense jawline, that appears more chiseled with his bright, contagious smile that matches his sparkling ocean blue eyes.

And Wade. Well, he's wearing his broodiness like a second skin, but the passion behind his eyes is as clear as Jasper's. The slight squint in his eyes and quirk in his lip gives him away. And I love knowing that I'm one of the few people that can read him like that.

As I appraise them, men and women spread to the sides as they trek up the walkway. They each pull out a bouquet of roses from behind their backs and hold it in front of their bodies as they walk toward me.

My jaw drops at the same time a beaming smile crosses my face, along with a flush of heat that I can't manage to control.

They step up to the booth and my nickname overlaps each of their greetings.

"Hey, princess."

"Hey, sweetheart"

"Hey, pumpkin."

Jasper's smile still adorns his gorgeous face as he glances over at Wade and Major, then back to me. "Truth or Dare?"

Giving the three of them a knowing look, my answer is easy.

"Triple dare."

EPILOGUE

ABBY

I throw my truck into park and jump out, racing toward the elevator. As the doors open, I squeeze through and wait impatiently as they retract. It's painfully slow as the doors merge together and finally starts to lift me to the seventh floor.

My foot taps anxiously as it ascends and I scold myself for not taking the stairs, because I have far too much nervous energy to stand here right now.

They came for me.

They showed up… for me. The idea of them pining over me as much as I did them sends an unexplainable thrill through my body.

I've spent the last week regretting how I left, confused by feelings I couldn't understand.

Not only was I hurting from the loss of my friend—a betrayal that completely blindsided me—but I was working through the loss of what felt like something so special.

One day in that fire house with them set my soul on fire, and it shouldn't have affected me the way it did. The sudden desire for more confused me. It made me feel like I was being stupid and careless. Throwing myself out there, just to get hurt again.

Taking it out on them was completely unfair, but I was embarrassed and had no idea how to feel about everything.

But, I have every intention of making it up to them now.

I can't help but smile as the elevator doors finally open for what felt like the longest elevator ride in history. I probably should have waited for them in the parking lot, but I wanted a few minutes to pick up my house and freshen up a little. Plus, there's something about opening your door to someone you invited over as opposed to walking through it with them.

Stepping out, I head toward my door taking the keys out of my purse. When I glance back up, I stop dead in my tracks.

"Sam?" I say questioningly.

He's sitting on the ground in front of my door, slouched with his head tipped back.

If he's not drunk, he's definitely hungover.

"Hey, baby." His voice is scratchy and sounds as wrecked as he looks.

"Not your baby. You need to leave." I look over my shoulder at the elevator. "Now."

Leaning over, he presses onto his palms and stands, taking his slow, sweet ass time. That is one thing I remember about him. He never had a sense of urgency when it came to time management. I was always waiting for him to fix his hair or change his outfit. It was insufferable.

"Sam, seriously. You need to leave and never come back. Go bother Cami or Sienna or whoever else you were seeing behind my back." I step toward my front door but he side steps, blocking me.

I clench my fists as I trail my gaze up his body. When my eyes meet his, there's a glossy sheen that coats them, laced with an anger that scares me.

He was never violent when we were together; but I guess they never are, until they don't get what they want.

I want to punch him, push him, force him to leave but I'm afraid of what might happen if I do.

"Abby—" he begins but the elevator dings, interrupting him.

We both look down the hall as Jasper steps out of the elevator. He's looking in the opposite direction as he scans the numbers, then turns our way seeing Sam and I standing in front of my door.

Jasper almost always has a smile on his face. It might not be a full-teeth grinning smile, but his eyes have a welcoming kindness that makes it seem like he's always happy.

The slight smirk that's usually a permanent fixture on his face vanishes, along with the warmth in his irises as he slowly tilts his head, as if he's trying to make sense of what he's seeing.

Sam opens his mouth but no words come out as Wade and Major's heads pop out of the elevator. They look incredulously in our direction before they step forward, standing on either side of Jasper.

And... wow.

I guess I say that out loud because Sam gives me a disgusted face as he turns to look down at me.

These men are imposing in the best way. They look as much the strong firefighters they are even without all the gear, and I can't help the wide grin that forms over my face.

"Isn't that the guy from the Farmer's Market?" Sam whispers, as if it's a secret between us. Stale alcohol wafts through the air between us and I step back waving my hand in front of my face.

"Wait a minute," Sam finally realizes. "Is he here for you? Are *they* here for you? Who are these guys?" He turns to look at me and I'm still smiling.

Standing tall, I lift my chin proudly, as I claim them. "My boyfriends."

Sam's face falls, then turns to look at my guys. All of them are smiling, even Wade, who seems to wear it the loudest.

Major begins to walk toward us. "You're not welcome here. *Ever*." He exaggerates the last word. "Don't ever set foot in this building again, and don't ever think about trying to get in touch with Abby. Don't call. Don't text. Email. Slide into her DM's," he says coolly. "None of it." He steps closer, then mouths '*ever*' once again.

He glances down at me, a smirk behind those irises that eats me up and nothing, not even a half-drunk Sam, can kill this smile.

Sam checks his surroundings, glances down at me, then back to all of them. And because he doesn't know how to stand up to anyone that isn't a woman, he hangs his head and steps around me. His shoulders slouch as he heads away from the elevator and toward the emergency exit stairwell.

Sam takes one look back at us. Anger laces his face but he silently turns his gaze to the floor, then disappears behind the metal door as it closes with a resounding thud.

Major turns back to me, cups my face and asks, "Are you okay?"

His touch is comforting and warm. I can't help but sigh a breath of relief as I close my eyes, nodding. And not necessarily because I was worried about Sam. I just missed his touch.

When I reopen them, they're all staring at me with an admiration I can't describe. A need and desire I've never felt from one man before, much less three.

"I know you guys aren't really my boyfriends, but I wanted to—"

"Oh, we're your boyfriends, princess." Major says, his voice confident but soft, claiming me just as easily as I claimed them. "We've already talked about all this—" He gestures his finger between Jasper, Wade and himself. "We were just waiting for you to get on board."

I bite my lip to smother the unavoidable smile creeping across my face.

I mean, California is known for their warmer winters, but is the AC broken in here or did my firemen just light me on fire? Because I might combust.

"Want to come in?" I ask, but duh, that's why they're here.

"Uh, yes. Yes, we do," Jasper answers for all of them.

JASPER

We step through the doorway into Abby's condo, and I swear I feel like it's my first time all over again.

Major and Wade were quiet on the drive over to the Farmers Market, and I knew they were feeling just as nervous as I was.

She could have turned us down. She could have decided what we had on Christmas Eve was just a fling, nothing more. But she felt it all. Just like we did.

The idea that the four of us can be something more, more than *Truth or Dare* or a *Guess Who* game hidden in the back of a fire station garage, makes me feel both exhilarated and fearful at the same time.

I'm already afraid to lose what we have, but so excited to see where it will lead. Out of the three of us, I've always been the one voted most likely to scream YOLO, and run down the street buck naked for funsies. No matter the challenge, I'm all in, heart on the table and soul exposed to the world.

Never once have I felt scared of the hurt it could cause.

This though.

This is something so goddamn special, and I'm already terri-fied to lose whatever we're starting.

I look between the three of them. Major stoically glances around the room taking in the surroundings as he normally does anywhere we go. Wade has his guard down, something I realized only Abby brings out in him anytime she's near, and Abby nibbles on the inside of her cheek as she gives us the tour of her home.

"It's not much," she says shyly.

"It's perfect. It's exactly what I thought your home would look like," Major replies as he steps toward her seeing that she needs comforting.

"Are you really okay?" he asks.

She nods. "Just nervous, I think. The three of you here. It's overwhelming."

We all stiffen at her confession.

"In a good way," she quickly clarifies. "Overwhelming in the best way ever."

Thank fucking god.

I sigh an obvious breath of relief. We all do.

"What do we do now?" She asks the question we all have been trying to figure out since we decided at the fire station that we were coming for her. We didn't know what the outcome would be or what the options were. All we knew was that we wanted Abby and it was up to her to decide where this went.

"What do you want?" I ask.

She looks between the three of us. "Everything."

MAJOR

Taking the lead, I step forward, cupping one hand around her face and gripping her hip with the other. I pull her into me because I've been thinking of nothing but her and the four of us for the last seven days. Recurring thoughts of what this could be and how we can make it work.

Lifting her chin, my lips graze over hers as I breathe her in. She still smells like candied apples and citrus, but that spicy mint mixture that Wade and Jasper added is missing.

"Come over here and kiss our girl," I tell them as I tease my lips over hers.

Jasper is the first to step toward us. Well, jump really.

He leaps in our direction, wrapping his hand around the nape of her neck and pulls her into him. Their moans are loud and needy as I continue to hold her close to me. I move my hand so both are now holding her hips as Wade steps on the other side of us. He cups her cheek and gently pulls her away from Jasper, smirking as he locks eyes with him, then leans in and kisses our girl.

"Mmmm, so good. So, so good." His words muffled through his needy kiss.

Jasper's eyes flicker between the two of them and I can't help my lopsided grin. The energy these two spent fighting against each other is now going to shift to fighting for her. And just as I predicted, Jasper leans in, stealing her lips away from Wade.

He crowds me too, stepping into my space as he replaces my hands with his and easily lifts her up. Her legs wrap around his waist as he heads toward the bedroom.

Opening the first door, he groans under her lips when he realizes it's a bathroom then steps back and reaches for the next door. He grunts when it opens outward seeing a line of linen and storage items.

"Oh, come on. Is your bedroom on the other side of the country or what?"

She tosses her head back and giggles, breaking the kiss, then flings her thumb over her shoulder. "Last door on the left."

"Did I say you can stop kissing me?" Jasper asks, but doesn't give her a chance to respond as he slides his hands behind her head, pulling her close again.

Wade shakes his head with an eye roll, which isn't unusual, but this time it accompanies a rare smile that I wish Jasper could see.

They make it to her bedroom and he's already laying her down on a miniature bed as we walk through the doorway.

Okay, it's not *that* small. But it will be a struggle fitting one of us on that bed, much less all three of us.

"Do you think we can fit two king beds in here?" Wade asks, hijacking my exact thoughts.

My eyes bounce around the room and I nod.

"We definitely need to get her a new bed, stat," I reply.

"With bedposts," he adds.

"Carved with our names on each one."

"Best idea I've ever heard," he agrees as he steps one foot forward, then uses the other to hold the back of his heel, removing his shoe. He does the same with the other foot then shrugs off his jacket, draping it over the arm of a chair placed in the corner of her room.

Well, isn't that convenient.

I walk over to it and sit down. It's beige and plush with buttons along the seams and incredibly comfortable.

Just another thing that was meant to be.

Unzipping my pants, I reach under the fabric and grip my already hard cock. It's been a long week without any kind of sexual activity and, while that hasn't been unusual for me in the past, I've been desperately craving more of this since Christmas Eve.

It's like Abby's presence opened up the flood gates for every one of our sexual desires, and now that we've had a taste, there's no going back.

Jasper is already naked, *not surprising*, and Abby is close behind wearing nothing but a barely-there thong. She scoots herself back on the bed as Jasper prowls above her, tucking his fingers at the waistband of the thin fabric as he strips the lace down her legs.

An animalistic growl radiates from his chest as he takes in her naked body. His eyes are solely focused at the apex of her thighs, already glistening and so fucking wet.

He glances over his shoulder, seeing Wade unbuttoning his pants, then tosses her panties in his face.

Wade's hand whips up to catch them and inhales, taking in her scent with a greedy hum.

A blush blooms on her cheeks as she nibbles on that gorgeous, plump bottom lip of hers and I can't help but moan at the sight.

"Get naked, she needs us." Jasper tells Wade, just before he dives face first into Abby.

He flattens his tongue, swiping at her center and Abby gasps as she flops back on the bed, flailing her arms out to her sides. She's got a white knuckle grip on her comforter as Jasper continues licking and sucking, moaning into her slick pussy.

"I've got to get you ready for us, pumpkin." He pushes one finger in as his eyes gaze up from between her legs. "Do you want that? Both of us at the same time?" he asks, in between circling his tongue over her clit as he pushes a second finger into her.

Her neck cranes up, looking down to meet his gaze and she nods with a feral look in her eyes.

Wade tucks her panties into his front pocket, then pulls out condoms from the back pocket of his pants, tossing them on the bed. He urgently strips, kicking off his pants and tearing off his shirt using just one hand.

Occupational benefit, I suppose. Quick dress and undress.

In less than thirty seconds Wade is naked, pressing his knee into the mattress as he leans into Abby. He begins kissing her ear, jaw, and then her lips as she moans through the four finger stroking that Jasper is feeding her.

"You're ready. You're so fucking ready," Jasper says in a hurry as he pushes himself up, wraps his arms around Abby's waist then pulls her onto him as he lays flat on the mattress.

She straddles Jasper as Wade kneels behind her and, fucking hell, the sight will be seared to my memory.

When she glances back at me, her eyes are full of lust and need, and my cock pulses a bead of precum at how incredible she looks. I grip my cock, attempting to reel myself in, when Abby leans down and kisses Jasper. As she pulls away she grabs the condoms then kicks her leg up and over Jasper, placing her back toward him, straddling him in reverse.

She tilts her face up toward Wade as he leans down and kisses her. Her fingers make quick work on the foil wrapper, tearing it open. Pulling out the latex, she tosses the wrapper to the side then pulls away from the kiss. I'm lost in a state of dèjá vu when she sucks the tip in between her lips and gazes up at Wade with those sultry brown eyes.

"Jesus Christ," I huff out in a whisper as I recall how she looked up at me with those same chocolate oval eyes, before taking me down her throat as she sheathed me.

Wade's hands fly onto his hips as she does the same to him, cupping her hand around the base of his cock as she uses that expert mouth of hers to put his condom on.

She pushes his cock deep down her throat, covering him completely. He hisses, inhaling heavily as Jasper watches them with a desperation that mirrors mine.

Satisfied, she pulls back, keeping her eyes locked on Wade's as she tears open the second wrapper with her teeth then holds the rim, sticking the tip out in Wade's direction.

"Your turn."

"Oh, fuck." Jasper's eyes widen as he holds onto Abby's waist with a death-like grip as if it will keep him grounded.

Wade looks between Abby and Jasper, then down at the thin latex tip. Leaning forward he takes it between his teeth, not taking his eyes off Abby.

She scoots back, gripping the base of Jasper's erect cock, lining it up for Wade. Jasper hisses, the whites in his knuckles growing as he hums like he's trying to distract himself.

"Oh god, fuck," Jasper bellows, his entire body jerking. "What the fuck?"

Tipping his head up, his eyes widen as he stares down at himself and through Abby's bent leg to see Wade bobbing up and down on his cock, holding the condom between his fingers.

"Jesus Christ. Wade, what are you doing?"

Wade hollows his cheeks and pops off the tip. "Easier to slide on your cock if it's wet," Wade replies with ease, like he didn't just send Jasper into another universe.

The tip of Jasper's cock leaks and Wade leans down, licks it like a lollipop, then covers it with the latex, using his mouth to roll it all the way down.

"Fuck, fuck, fuck," Jasper bangs his head against the pillow. "I'm not going to last long." Jasper sounds angry, but the needy groan that radiates from his chest completely negates all the frustrated profanities he was just muttering when Wade holds Jasper's cock upright at the base as Abby lifts her hips, and lowers herself over Jasper's length.

"Fuuuucccckk." Jasper spits out as he squeezes his eyes closed.

Abby begins moving her hips in a rocking motion as if she competed in the Olympics for professional hip rolling.

I can't help but stroke my leaking cock as I watch her hips magically rock over his, taking the full length of his cock while Wade strokes himself. My eyes bounce between all of them, taking in this beautiful and filthy sight, and I'm filled with so much lust and need and desire.

How did I—did we—get so lucky to have whatever it is that we're building right now? I worked hard at my marriage, attempted to be anything and everything I could to make my wife happy. I sacrificed more of myself for my ex. But *this*, this all feels natural and so perfect, and I make a promise to myself to cherish it and take care of her, them, all of us. Because *this* is everything.

Wade glances over at me, taking me in. He matches my tempo, as if it's a way for him to make me feel like I'm next to them, playing with them. But I don't need that, not right now. I just want to see all of their pleasure. I want to see them fall apart.

Jasper's moans are loud and ascending right along with Abby's. An almost invisible smirk crosses over Wade's face as he steps to the side of the bed, dragging his hand across Abby's jaw, down her collarbone, before he cups her breast, massaging her nipple between his thumb and finger. She must clench harder around Jasper because his mouth falls open along with hers. Jasper's eyes trail up Wade's colossal form, now standing directly over him.

Leaning forward, he grips the headboard, lines his cock up with Jasper's slacked jaw and pushes the tip over his lips and down his throat.

Jasper moans around his cock, taking everything Wade is giving him, and Abby whimpers as her hooded eyes watch them from over her shoulder.

"Fuck," I spit out, stroking harder.

Jasper continues to groan, saliva dripping from around his lips and over Wade's cock as he thrusts into his mouth.

"That's it, get my cock nice and wet, Jas. I want to feel every ridge of your cock when I slide into our girl."

Jasper grunts and hums, almost as if he needs to confess all his sins.

My cock pulses with Wade's dirty words and the soundtrack of heavy breathing, so I know Jasper is on the precipice of losing his fucking mind.

"Are you ready for them, princess?" I ask as I push myself off the chair and walk toward them.

WADE

I'm so glad Major is stepping in with us now. I've been thinking of this moment nonstop for the past week and I want us all joined during our first time together. That makes it feel complete.

Major stands next to me as I move back to my position in between Abby and Jasper's legs. A sight that I swear I'll never get over. To see the cock I've been craving slide in and out of our dream girl.

It's fucking priceless.

My cock glistens with my own precum mixed with Jasper's saliva—yet another timeless view—and I give myself another long languid stroke.

Gently pressing my other palm into Abby's breastbone, I slowly lean her back as I line myself up with her entrance.

They both still as I push in the tip. I can't help but groan as her pussy swallows the crown and grips me with a force I can't put into words. I freeze as a shiver rolls through my entire body before I suck in a deep breath and slide further into her, massaging the backside of Jasper's cock.

The collective gasps and moans that follow are otherworldly.

"Oh, fuck," Abby whines.

"Fucking hell, that's good," Jasper confesses like a prayer.

"Mmmm, so tight," I grit out.

"Open up for me, princess," Major says with an urgency like he's unable to wait any longer.

She immediately obeys as her mouth drops open. She flattens her tongue and he pushes his hard cock into her delicious mouth, thrusting his hips in a punishing tempo as Jasper and I do the same to her pussy.

"This is what heaven feels like," Jasper manages to say as he drives into her. Stroking both her walls and my cock with expert precision.

"You were made for us, sweetheart," I confess easily, because I've never felt so strongly about anyone before. No one has brought out what she has in me, Jasper or Major. I take in the view of all of us and this is exactly how it should be.

"You're ours," Major says, still fucking her face but with a softness and power that only he can perfect.

She pulls away from Major moaning loudly, as her teeth bite into my skin and her fingertips score into the flesh of my forearms. Her pussy clenches around our cocks, and Jasper's vein pulses against the backside of my own, pushing me over the edge.

"Fuck, I'm coming," I groan, erupting in waves in some sort of synchronized manner alongside Jasper.

"Princess," Major whispers with a desperation I don't normally hear.

Abby shifts her gaze toward him, taking in Major's wanton body. His begging eyes are hooded, his jaw slack, and the crown of his cock is thinned and pink, ready to explode.

Abby opens her mouth, leans forward and takes him in as he roars through his orgasm. He comes and comes; it's loud and messy and the view of us all wrecked for each other is a sight that will never get old.

Major pulls back, gasping, as he leans down to catch his breath.

Abby lifts herself off Jasper and lays down next to him. I kneel down, melting into the end of the bed, giving my body a much needed reprieve.

"Fuck," Jasper says like he's still in shock.

"That was... unbelievable," Abby confesses and we all hum in agreement.

A few minutes pass before Major finally stands and goes to the bathroom to clean up. Jasper goes next, then me.

I remove the condom, tie it at the top and use toilet paper to wrap it up. I toss it in the trash can and take in the site of both Jaspers condom and mine laying at the bottom of the wastebasket.

Is it horrible that I hate the idea of using them? This is it, for me at least, and this is just another way to show them how all-in I am. I'm going to suggest we all get tested and go bare. I want to feel everything with them and I don't want anything between us.

I finish washing my hands and grab a purple hand towel from the rack. I soak it in warm water, ring it out then head back into her room.

I don't know who started the conversation but clearly they were thinking the same thing I was about protection.

"I was tested after Sam, when I found out he had been cheating. Thankfully, it was negative. I haven't been with anyone since," she says, turning her gaze to Jasper.

"I got tested last week." He wiggles his eyebrows and glances over at Major with a self-satisfying grin.

"Well, I had no idea you guys were going from 0-to-100 so quickly. In fact, up until yesterday, I had no idea I even had a team anymore." He glares over at the two of us who went MIA on him last week.

I feel bad about that. But disconnecting from them put everything into perspective for me, so I have no regrets.

I make my way through the landscape of clothing strewn all over the floor and sit on the bed next to Abby. Using the washcloth, I give her a soft sponge bath, wiping down the front of her chest, down her torso and over her center, taking my time because I love taking care of her.

Major turns his gaze to me. "Wade?"

I don't look up. I just focus on Abby, but I know I need to answer the question.

"The last test I took, I was positive for chlamydia." I swallow thickly as all three of them look in my direction. "My ex, she cheated, too." I peer over at Abby, giving her a sympathetic smile, because I know exactly how devastating that feels. "I got a single dose antibiotic then got retested and everything came back clear. That was almost two years ago… and I haven't slept with anyone since."

"Oh, shit." Jasper leans forward. "Two years?" he asks. "You mean to tell me that when I jerked you off last week, that was the first time someone else touched your cock in almost two years?"

My eyes widen as I glare at him.

"Wait, what?" Abby sits up. "Did you guys hook up before we all did?"

"Hell yeah we did, and it was *hot*," Jasper confesses happily exaggerating the word hot like it sizzled his tongue just saying it.

"I knew something happened," Major whispers to himself as he stands, "I don't even want to know," Major says as he shakes his head and joins us all on the bed.

"You guys are going to tell me about that later," Abby whispers to Jasper and I with a pointed look.

"Are we all really going to do this? A relationship together?" Major asks, his voice strong and confident as usual but, as his eyes look between the three of us, they're laced with concern. Like he's afraid that what is happening right now might not be real.

No one answers, even though I know damn well what Major and Jasper want. And, I know exactly what I want. We just want Abby to take the lead on this one. It's up to her. We all agreed, it's her choice.

But what if she wants just Jasper because he's carefree and easy going? Or maybe she wants to explore a relationship with Major, who's stable and reliable. Neither come with the baggage I do.

Just then, she leans over the bed and reaches for her phone that lays on top of the nightstand.

"Scooch in. All of you." Jasper velcros himself to her left side, while I lay down on her right. Major crawls in between as she holds her phone up in a selfie position and snaps a photo of the four of us, grinning from ear-to-ear.

It's one simple shot, yet it somehow turns out perfect. She taps on her screen and the keyboard pops up. She types just one simple hashtag then hits *post*, for the entire world to see.

#myguys

MORE FROM THE AUTHOR

Please check out these other titles by Berlin Wick. The e-books are available on Kindle and the DUET narrated audiobooks can be found on all audio platforms, including for direct download on the authors website at www.berlinwick.com

<u>The Secrets We Hide</u>
MFM
Voyeur Husband
Billionaire Boss

<u>The Promises We Break</u>
Drunken Vegas Wedding turned
Marriage of Convenience
Pro Baseball Player

<u>The Games We Play</u>
Second Chance Romance
Grumpy/Sunshine
Ex-Navy Seal / Yoga Instructor
Neighbors

ACKNOWLEDGMENTS

For me, this is typically one of the hardest parts to write. There are so many people that I need to acknowledge as an author, wife, mom, friend and reader.

Due to the context of Lettuce Turnip the Beet with our FMC being a former corporate world employee who left it all to focus solely on content creation, let's start there. Obviously, that is not something we can all do, but I think we dream of doing it. At least in some form or another. Either by way of alpha/beta reading or editing full time. PA or cover design. Perhaps writing or narrating full time. As great as it sounds, IT IS A LOT OF HARD WORK. Staying self-motivated to do what you need to do to get exposed, figuring out algorithms and what works. Diving into what is trending. Keeping up with the ever changing technology and new features. A majority of the people I know are wives, moms and work full time. So, kudos to you to find time to do this. With that being said, there are so many people in the bookstagram and booktok world that have helped me along the way, I could write another book on just listing your names. So many of you consistently create content on my books, make the funniest, most entertaining reels, create content graphics, share quotes and drive so many readers in our direction. **Please know**, if you have posted about one of my books, made a reel or story, commented and/or shared any of my content, YOU are included in this. Because if it weren't for you I wouldn't have the joy of writing or the joy of meeting other readers and writers that I adore so much. SO, THANK YOU. Thank you for supporting me on this crazy journey. I appreciate you more than you know.

My amazing Betas, what would I do without you??? Kelly, Susan, Courtney, Amanda, Madison and Tyleigh. Thank you for input, guidance, love and feedback.

Kristin Barrett and your amazing vision. Thank you for designing the most fitting cover! Somehow you understood my mess of words as I tried to explain my Firefighter reverse harem booked called "Lettuce Turnip the Beet" and ran with it. This cover is absolutely perfect!

Kay Morton, AKA: Editor, Hawkeye, word fixer extraordinaire! Thank you for making sense of my terrible grammar!

My friends… My family. This topic means a lot to me. My immediate 'family' is very small. However, the friends I have in my life have become my family. Found family is truly a main trope for my personal life. You guys have supported me, cheered me on and have been my biggest fans. Thank you for everything. I would do anything for you guys.

My boys. You get whiplash dealing with my overly loving side and that batshit crazy side. My oldest is starting college and out of the house. Thank you for checking in and asking how my book stuff is going, but please GOD, please don't read them. My youngest, I will always and forever be the 'time manager' and when you are older and read this (let's hope not), I know you will be just like me in that regard. Mark my words, little one.

And last, but not least, my amazing, supportive, loving husband. I have said before and I'll say it again. You are truly one of the good ones. Thank you for taking care of me, being my loudest cheerleader, allowing me to do what I love and genuinely supporting me through every step of it. You are my real life book boyfriend.

ABOUT THE AUTHOR

Berlin was raised in a tiny town in North Idaho who moved to the Bay Area, California, at the age of eighteen. She now resides in San Diego with her husband, two boys and her massive Cane Corso named Blu! Her bucket list items include skydiving, attending the Oscars, becoming a New York Time best-selling author, and cruising the world for retirement. She loves writing and reading, ANY and ALL kinds of romance novels, and loves engaging in the booksta community. You can find her most active on Instagram!